ISBN: 978-1-998763-45-0

For Ramona. You'll always be my big sexy sasquatch.

TROG

Zachary Ashford

PROLOGUE

In the tunnels beneath his home, Roger Shackleton approached the beast. The hulking shape loitered in the back of the cavern, visible by the flickering firelight of Shackleton's torch.

The problem with imprisoning it in these subterranean tunnels was the redolent smell of piss had nowhere to go. The musty stench permeated the still air. Acrid, biting, to be frank, disgusting. Shackleton held his pre-prepared jar of vinegar to his nose and sniffed, trying to clear his head. He raised the torch, and orange light cast the huge creature in the palettes of hell. The monster flinched away from the torch's radiance, growling softly. Its eyes were no doubt accustomed to darkness after so long in this stygian prison.

Thankfully, the gigantic, hairy creature,

some sort of throwback to a time between ape and man, had fallen easily for the trap Shackleton had set. It had been baited simply enough in the deep forests of the region, but getting it down to these caverns, through the guano-laden tunnels, beyond the dynamite-blasted passageways, and into the stygian darkness of the cave had proved to be a monumental challenge. Seven of his employees had died, and the others had required significant bribes to even contemplate the task he set them, and then they too had died. At Shackleton's hand.

Finally, though, the beast was a secure captive, secreted away in a place where it could not escape while he made his preparations. He had stumbled on the caverns of this region while searching for somewhere to stake his claim on land.

The Government needed men who were prepared to till the fields, turn the earth, grow crops, and domesticate the wild environs of this country at the bottom of the world. Shackleton had no plans to manage a farm himself, though. No, he would bring a miraculous travelling sideshow to the colonies, while profiting from the guano filling these caves. With it as a source of income, he could happily pay a ranch manager to take care of the mundane tediousness of farming.

For him, it would be the life of the freak show. He was a performer, a traveller from way back, and if he could tame this hideous missing link, he'd strike it rich.

"I take it you're hungry," he said, knowing already the monster, which the natives would refer to as a hairy man, would be the star of the show. He already had the advertising hoardings painted: a great hairy man to rival the sasquatches, yetis, and bigfoots of the Americas and Asia, holding a damsel in distress in its gigantic hand as it roared. The top of the image was adorned with the name he had chosen for the beast: Trog!

Unfortunately, domesticating Trog was proving a far from simple proposition. As it loitered in the back of the cavern, watching him with suspicious eyes, Shackleton knew the monster would happily snap his neck, even if such a move would damn it to spend all eternity down here, either living off the bats calling these caverns home, or starving in its prison.

Shackleton slipped the torch into its sconce and stepped away from the light. He withdrew a loaf of bread from the bag he'd brought with him and tore a hunk free.

"Come, eat some bread, Trog." Daring to poke his arm through the cage, he offered the morsel.

The beast made a low growling noise. It reverberated off the stone walls and resonated in the pit of Shackleton's stomach.

In response, he cooed at the monster. "It's okay. Trust me. I don't want to harm you. I want to make you famous."

He tossed the bread, and Trog watched it bounce harmlessly on the floor without touching it, then levelled his suspicious eyes on Shackleton.

Shackleton tore himself a thin strip of the bread and popped it into his own mouth, exaggerating the taste by patting his stomach and making noises of satisfaction.

The monster picked the piece from the ground, sniffed it, and then bit down. It chewed, never taking its glare off the man who'd imprisoned it, and swallowed.

Another hunk of bread.

It plucked this offering from the air and scarfed it down, still watching Shackleton with wariness.

Shackleton took another chunk of the bread. This time, he didn't throw it, he only offered it. "Well done, Trog. Good boy. Come and get it."

Trog growled.

"It's okay, Trog. We're friends, you and I." Shackleton wasn't exactly sure of it, but he hoped repeating the creature's name and speaking to it softly would make it like him. After all, if he was going to use the creature in the travelling freak show, he'd need to be sure it wouldn't harm anybody. And, given the fact this particular attraction wouldn't just be a weirdo, but a bona fide cryptid, he'd need to be certain it was completely docile. If it ever hurt anyone, it would be the end of him and his sideshow—which meant working a life of labour, probably carting wheelbarrows full of batshit, in the ridiculous heat of Central Queensland.

The monster edged closer, still growling, but not as emphatically.

"That's it, Trog, that's it. Come on."

Shackleton extended his arm as far forward as he could, proffering the bread.

Trog reached out a finger the size of a human forearm and plucked the bread free. He ate it, scampering out of reach.

Shackleton was ecstatic. Maybe training this damned thing would be easier than he'd previously considered. "Good boy, Trog! This is called bread. Can you say bread?"

Trog said nothing, but edged forward, reaching out to yet another piece of bread while growling so quietly it sounded almost like he was purring.

"Bread," Shackleton said. "Bread!"

Trog closed a vicelike hand firmly around Shackleton's wrist. Roared. The hot mist of his breath washed over Shackleton.

He winced as the beast applied pressure. "Let go, Trog! Let go!"

But Trog only squeezed tighter.

Shackleton pissed his pants as his captive applied pressure. His pleas became screams. The bones in his wrist began to crunch and crack within the strong grip of Trog's primitive hand. The grinding sounds only excited the monster further.

It bellowed, gobs of foaming saliva dripping from its gums, and with a grunt, it yanked Shackleton's arm as hard as it could.

Shackleton smashed into the iron bars of Trog's purpose-built prison. His feet left the ground as Trog pulled, stretching his arm first upwards, and then tightly against the bars. He could only watch in horror as Trog reached through the bars and grabbed the back of his head.

Screaming, crying, howling, Shackleton rued killing the workers who'd helped him catch the beast. If their bodies weren't stacked in a neat pile inside the enclosure, they might have been able to help. As things were, he could only beg. "No, Trog! No! Bad Trog!"

Trog grasped Shackleton's head with both hands and pulled as hard as he could, trying to squeeze it through the iron bars like one might try to pull a knotted shoelace through an eyelet.

The wrought iron prison held.

Shackleton's head split three ways around the two iron bars. His eyes popped. His brains oozed. A chunk of skull fell to the floor with a wet slap.

———

When Trog was done feasting on the exposed brain, he realized he couldn't pull the larger parts of the girthy man's corpse through and resorted to tearing him limb from limb, bringing him through piece by piece. He sucked the bloody ichor from his fingers and chewed on the flesh.

It didn't matter if he was trapped. He had food, and with the continual running water dripping from the cave's ceiling, he was never at risk of dehydration. Sooner or later, someone else would find him, or the earth would shift, and he would be free to roam the forests again.

CHAPTER ONE

Aisha Solomon barely heard her parents calling. She was too busy resting comfortably on her plush bed, swiping her way through social media, and twirling her hair as she listened to the latest single from Hailey Comma, her favourite popstar.

If her folks wanted to head out for the night, having a boring dinner with boring people, leaving her in this probably haunted house they'd decided to buy in the middle of nowhere, she would stay in her room, where she didn't have to think about the fact all her friends were in the city, miles away from Shackleton, the dead little township Dad had insisted on dragging her to.

The door to her room rattled. When the handle didn't turn, whoever was on the other side, pounded on it. BANG! BANG! BANG!

"Aisha! Open up!"

She rested her tablet on her pillow and got up with a groan. Her dad was so annoying.

"I told you not to lock the door," he said as she pulled it slightly open.

"Sorry," she replied, trying not to tell him he knew why the door was locked. Life might have returned to normal, but she would never be trapped behind an unlocked door again.

"We're going in five. Your mum wants to show you how the gas cooker works."

"I know how the gas cooker works. You turn it on, and flames come out."

"Not quite. Get down there and see your mum. And turn your music down. The poor girl sounds like she's got a mouthful of marbles. Don't singers these days know mumbling isn't singing?"

"Whatever, Dad. Just because our performing artists aren't passing out drunk and drowning on their own vomit every five minutes doesn't make them any less valid."

"If you say so," Dad said, rolling his own eyes, "but Dave Williams would be spinning in his grave if he heard what you lot call music nowadays."

Aisha laughed. Her Dad's obsession

with a very specific era in nu metal always made for interesting conversations about music with her peers. Most of her friends had normal parents who thought the biggest and best bands in music were the likes of Coldplay, Imagine Dragons, and the Foo Fighters. Her old man would have none of it, and on the few occasions he'd driven the car-pool to school, back when they'd lived in civilisation and public appearances were still a part of her daily life, he'd blasted them with bands like Trapt, Powerman 5000, Dry Kill Logic, and Spineshank. The stuff was terrible, but he loved it. He was quirky and weird, and although he was probably ten per cent more annoying than any other dad, she loved him all the same, even if it had been hard to put into words lately. She still hadn't forgiven him for moving her out to the bush just when she had worked up the nerve to start attending school again.

Her Mum couldn't have been more

different to him, and Aisha had no idea how they'd ended up dating. She was into classical music and played the piano. When Dad told everyone, unironically, Static X were the greatest band the world had ever seen, her Mum would make vomit gestures and laugh. She wasn't sure how Mum felt about the move, but considering Dad's job was supposed to be paying well, the answer was more than likely completely quantifiable.

Aisha entered the kitchen to find her Mum mulling over the carton of red wine or the carton of white wine. "Dad says you want to show me how the gas oven works."

"It's high time you learned, and with no Dominos Pizza out here in the sticks, the time is now!"

Aisha's heart dropped. "Can't we just order Pizza Hut or get Uber Eats or something?"

Mum laughed. "No, there's no Dominos, there's no Pizza Hut, there's no

Uber Eats, there's not even a McDonalds unless you want to walk all the way out to the highway—and they don't deliver this far off the beaten track. Welcome to the sticks!" She plopped the carton of red on the bench.

Dad's ridiculous idea to move away from the city for a 'tree-change' was now *officially* the worst thing she'd ever experienced. Sure, he had taken a job with the Department of Environment, and they needed him to explore some long-abandoned caves in the area around the house, and it would make his commute a lot shorter and easier, but she wondered why he hadn't just continued to work away from home on a fly-in fly-out basis. It had always worked in the past.

"Can we please move back to the city?"

Mum looked at her sadly. "'Fraid not, sweetheart. This is us now. Don't take it too hard. Once school starts, you'll get used to it."

"I still don't know why I couldn't finish grade eleven and twelve in the city while you live out here!"

"You know how we feel after...well, you know how we feel. *This is us now*."

Aisha didn't know why she bothered to complain. Dad just went weird on her, and she was pretty sure her Mum should get a 'THIS IS US NOW' tattoo on her forehead so she didn't have to keep repeating it."

"This house is creepy."

"I'll admit it's quirky."

Quirky? Last night, Aisha had heard something knocking far below the house. "With all those caves, and the weird, locked door under the house, this place is far beyond quirky."

"Stay away from the door under the house!"

Aisha rolled her eyes. She hadn't even known Dad was listening.

"There is no way I'm going near the

door, Dad. There's something down there, and I don't want to meet it. I heard it knocking and shouting again in the night while I was sleeping."

Dad looked at Mum with wide eyes. "It's just the Shackleton ghost," he said. "You do know the guy just disappeared and was never found, right? They say he haunts the old house to this day, trying to find his way back in."

Thankfully, Aisha saw him wink at Mum, because she would have believed him otherwise. She had *definitely* heard something last night, and although Dad slept like the world's most sedate baby, the look on Mum's face suggested she'd also heard the sounds.

"I'm serious, though, darling. Stay away from the door. It needs to be checked by engineers to ensure it's structurally sound before we explore it."

"Dad, I'm not going near the door." She'd found the door underneath the house while stacking tools. It had been partially submerged by mud and weeds due to a lack of maintenance. It hadn't been opened for a long time.

Good. It gave her the heebie-jeebies.

She'd first heard the strange bellowing from underground on the same day she'd found it. Dad had taken it upon himself to clear it of weeds and detritus, making jokes about the fact the house's previous owners might have been satanists, preppers, or even outback swingers with a purpose-built sex dungeon, but she didn't want to know what was down there. She didn't want to be anywhere near it. In fact, she wanted to be about 600km away from it, back in Brisbane with her friends, preparing for her final two years of schooling and making up for all the time she'd lost.

Still grinning about his latest 'funny,' Dad checked his watch. "Did you…?"

"Just about to," Mum said. "Come on, Aisha, let me show you how this stove works. We don't want you singeing your eyebrows off while we're out."

"What time are you coming back anyway?"

"We're meeting your father's new colleagues. We'll be late, no doubt."

Aisha groaned. As much as she didn't exactly want to hang out with her parents, she didn't want to be alone here, either. Especially after dark. If she heard strange bellowing coming from inside the mountain again, she might just have a heart attack.

CHAPTER TWO

Zombie popped the trunk and made sure the duffel bag was fully packed. He began to close the boot, then hesitated, retrieved the Glock from the bag and slipped it inside his inner pocket. The chances of cops stopping and searching out here were far beyond slim, so carrying the weapon wasn't a risk.

If there happened to be anyone out in the front yard of tonight's destination, he'd be prepared. The house was isolated, but if things went awry and they were surprised by a nosey neighbour, a good Samaritan, or even a late-night Amazon delivery, he would be a good boy scout and have his ducks in a row.

The gun might also serve another purpose: if Wolf, pissed him off enough, Zombie might just plug him before the end of the night. *It wouldn't be the worst thing in the world—a bigger cut of any money they found for one thing.* Still, as nice as it would be, it would just mean another body to dispose of when he was done. It would make extra work, and if Zombie was any kind of thrill killer, he was the efficient type.

He got into the driver's seat, checked to make sure his zombie mask was still in the glovebox from last time, slipped the keys into the ignition, and sparked the engine into life. "You guys ready for this?"

In response, the woman who would be wearing the skull mask nodded.

The guy wearing the wolf mask howled.

Zombie slapped the steering wheel with the heel of his hand. "I told you to cut it out. We're not here to mess about. We're here to do a job, exactly like we did last week. Get in, check the property for any signs of security, do the business, then get out without being seen, so quit playing around, and get your head right."

In the rearview mirror, Wolf tugged the mask off. "Bloody hell. I was just having a bit of fun."

Skull sighed but Zombie chose to ignore it. She was as sick of Wolf's bullshit as he was, but she was probably also over him chewing the guy out. *What were things coming to?*

Back when they first started tearing through random houses in regional towns and villages, it had been fun. They'd all been best mates. They'd enjoyed everything from the prep to the executions and the getaways to the media reports following their crimes. These days, things were more stressful, even if no one had a clue they were the ones who'd been racking up a mountain of kills in isolated towns.

They were always careful not to follow any pattern in town or suburb, making sure they randomly selected where to go next by pulling town names out of a hat, but with half a dozen houses ticked off and the families who lived in them executed, he had to wonder if guilt was weighing on any of them. He still felt cool about things, but while he was reasonably certain Wolf was too stupid to feel a complex emotion like guilt or regret, Skull gave him pause for thought.

Lately, she seemed different.

Zombie took a deep breath. "Wolf, I get it. We're all having a blast doing this but save the fun for when we get there. When we do, you can piss in all the corners, howl to your heart's content, and splatter brains around the place. For now, though. Let's play it cool. We need to be a normal crew out for a nice Sunday drive if we come across any random breathalysers or security stops."

Wolf picked his teeth. "I just get so keyed up beforehand, you know. Man, the last house, back in Goondiwindi...I still picture that kid's expression when I buried the axe in his face. He was so shocked!"

"In fairness, it was a one-in-a-million shot," Skull said.

"No way! I was practicing all week."

Zombie grinned. "Yeah, and you didn't hit the bullseye once."

Wolf beamed from ear to ear. "I'll make a champion axe-thrower yet, you'll see!" He hit Skull for a fistbump and buckled his seatbelt in. "Let's do this!"

Zombie shifted the car into gear, glad things were back on track. *It was going to be a good night.*

CHAPTER THREE

Aisha's parents were long-gone and she was holed up in her bedroom, behind a locked door. *Take that, Dad!*

She'd spent the last couple of hours chatting to her friends in the city via messenger and promising to come see them as soon as she could, but now it was time to watch NETFLIX and relax. Thankfully, the house had a good wireless connection. With the property being so far out of civilisation, she'd originally feared she'd have no way to stay connected to the internet, but unlike fast food, folks in the country considered good wireless a necessity. Considering their nearest neighbour was several kilometres away, she understood why.

She navigated to *Stranger Things*, then changed her mind. If she was in the middle of an intense moment, and heard something growling or knocking in the subterranean darkness below the house, she would die on the spot. Instead, she decided for something light and fluffy. What she needed right now was something with lots of sun, lots of surf, and lots of shirtless dumbasses. Moments later, she was leaning against her bedhead, watching manufactured drama unfold on *Love Island.*

She was chewing on a musk stick when the first bellowing sound of the night rumbled up from beneath the ground. Her heart beat a little faster, but she assured herself there was no such thing as monsters and ideas of the supernatural were for primitive people who lived long, long ago. Still, she paused her show, swiped her way onto Google and searched WHY DO CAVES MAKE GROANING SOUNDS?

As expected, there was a logical, scientific reason for it: water trapped in caves can drip, and due to the acoustics, it can produce a moaning sound. Perfect! It accounted for the knocking too. *God, she loved the internet!*

She went back to *Love Island*, thankful people as dumb as the ones on there were few and far between in the real world. When she hit play, the show stuttered, buffered, paused, and then disappeared. A message popped onto the screen. The wireless connection was dead.

What the hell?

After waiting a few minutes for it to reconnect, restarting her tablet, and checking to make sure she hadn't accidentally connected to some neighbour's connection (fat chance), it still hadn't returned. It was getting dark outside, and she flicked the light switch in the hallway as she made her way to the study where the modem was kept. It worked fine, so whatever the problem, the electricity was still good. If there was an internet outage, she was going to be spewing.

Someone was on the patio.

Looking inside the window.

Looking directly at her.

Someone wearing a zombie mask.

Aisha froze.

What the heck?

The figure in the zombie mask raised its hand and waved. Aisha didn't know what else to do. She waved back.

Then the zombie raised its other hand, revealing a knife, a big, jagged-looking knife like something out of a horror movie. *Holy shit, I'm going to die, and no one is going to be around to save me.* Sure, she'd locked up tight after Mum and Dad left, because of the noises from beyond the door beneath the house, and because she was still a fifteen-year-old girl and she wasn't stupid, but she still felt a desperate need to check the locks. Again!

Sprinting, she rattled the patio-door handle and double-checked the latches were secure.

THUMP! THUMP! THUMP!

The front door!

She ran, checking it. Safe.

Finally, the laundry door. All the doors were locked. *Thank you, past Aisha! Thank you, past trauma!*

Now, the phone. With no wireless, she had to hope there was signal out here *for the first time ever.* No dice, but her dad was a practical and pragmatic man. He'd installed a landline in the study.

She ducked in there. Lifted the handle.

Dead.

This was like one of those scary as hell home invasion movies. Some nutjob had come to murder her while her parents were gone. If she was cynical, she might have wondered if this was one of Dad's pranks, but even he wouldn't go this far. Mum wouldn't let him for one thing. He was annoying and over-sensitive and too busy blaming himself for things he couldn't control, but he wasn't evil. He wouldn't ever pull a prank like this.

Then something else occurred to her. She had been looking at the man in the zombie mask when she heard the knocking on the front door.

There must be two of them.

She peered out of the study and checked to see if the bloke was still there. He was. But he wasn't alone. There was a smaller figure wearing a skull mask beside him now. She held a knife also. She waved.

This time, Aisha didn't wave back. She slipped back into the study and pressed her body tight against the wall.

THUMP! THUMP! THUMP!

The front door again, but Zombie and Skull were both still on the patio at the back door. *There were three of them.* At least.

Fuck! Fuck! Double-fuck!

She had to think. How did people in movies get out of these circumstances? As the answer dawned on her, she realised it wasn't the one she wanted: they didn't. She was going to die. She was definitely going to die.

Her dad had to have something heavy in here, or something sharp, or threatening. The desk was bare. Stacks of paper, some pens, a calculator. Nothing capable of helping her. No weapons. Not even a pair of scissors.

The cupboard was limited also. Coat hangers? Jumpers? Belts and ties? *Why did Dad have to be such a pacifist?* If they were going to be country people, they should have some sort of rifle or shotgun ready at all times. *Didn't all country people have guns?*

The kitchen would be her next best bet. If she could get to the kitchen, she could grab a knife, maybe even the blowtorch her mum used for making crème brulé. First, though, she had to see if the weirdos outside had cut the line or if the modem needed a simple reset.

She hit the reset button, planning to get to the kitchen and back before checking it.

It always took a few seconds to reconnect. She hit the switch and bolted.

Zombie and Skull were gone when she ran into the hallway. She scanned the perimeter, hoping to catch a glimpse of them through an open window.

THUMP! THUMP! THUMP!

The front door again.

"Fuck off!" she screamed. "I've got a gun."

Whoever was at the front door howled. Literally, like a wolf. *They fucking howled.* Aisha started to shake. This was like something had taken the worst night of her life and pumped it full of steroids and methamphetamines. Her knees knocked. Her guts roiled. Her hands went clammy.

Focus, girl. Don't panic. Act. Don't get trapped again!

"Little girl," the howler screamed, "it doesn't matter if you don't open up, because I can HUFF and I can PUFF and I can BLOW YOUR DOOR IN!"

THUMP! THUMP! THUMP!

The blows were so powerful the whole house shook. Photos on the walls rattled. Something on the windowsill beside the door clattered to the ground.

She had to escape. Aisha had no illusions about the security of the house. She'd only recently heard Mum and Dad talking about the need to get security screens, cameras, and alarms. They had lived in a busy suburb in Brisbane where security was a necessity. Since they'd got here, Mum had been saying she felt naked without such precautions. Dad had been upset the contractors couldn't get out here sooner, and had even considered delaying the whole move because of it.

Aisha had thought the country would be safe, at least for a while. Yes, it had been a challenge, but she'd been confident things would be fine. She'd been wrong. Fighting back a panic attack, unable to see any of the strange mask-wearing lunatics who'd targeted the house, she realised they were toying with her. If they wanted to get through the windows, they could. If they wanted to smash the doors in, they could. Security was a necessity in the city and here. It was a mistake to move in without it.

The maniac at the front door howled again, long and loud.

Aisha grabbed a butcher's knife. Unable to find the blowtorch, she ransacked the shelves below the sink. There was bleach there, and bug-spray. If she could spray them or splash them with either of those, she could buy herself time. She'd seen *Home Alone* a hundred times in the last year, she could manage this situation until her parents came home. She had to.

SMASH!

Glass rained at the back patio. Laughter rang out.

Think, Aisha, think! Right now, there was someone at the front door. There were two people at the back door. The only other escape was the laundry door—or a window. The laundry door was too close to the patio, probably only five or six steps. She couldn't take the risk.

Mum and Dad's ensuite was the best choice. It was tucked away in the west side of the house, and if she could get in there, she could lock the master bedroom, the walk-in wardrobe, and the bathroom door itself before climbing out the window.

From there, she would have to take her chances, but if she stayed here, she was a fish in a barrel, and she knew what kinds of things could happen to lone girls trapped by home invaders.

More glass smashed and tinkled to the ground. They were breaking all the windows.

The man at the front door howled again. "You asked for it!" he screamed. And then, seconds later, a huge crunching sound boomed from the door. It swung violently open, and Aisha saw the man in the wolf mask. He was huge. He held a sledgehammer. It looked like the kind of weapon a Norse god would use. His shoulders must've been six-feet wide, and the bristles of his snarling mask almost touched the top of the doorframe.

"Boo!" he said. "Time to party!"

He dropped the hammer, and it clattered to the ground beside...*no fucking way*...a chainsaw.

Fuck fuck fuck fuck fuck!

Triple-fuck!

Aisha bolted to the master bedroom, knowing she didn't have time to check the wireless connection and slammed the door shut, locking it instantly.

The wolf-man howled again.

CHAPTER FOUR

Deep in the bowels of the caverns below the house, Trog cocked an ear. He hadn't heard this much noise coming from the land above in a long time. Had never heard the kinds of noises emanating now. The closest he could remember to sounds of this nature were the sounds of the men who'd chased him into the caves, who'd left him trapped in prison for so long.

He remembered it with immense sadness. He had forgotten the warmth of the sun and hadn't seen the outside world for so many sleeps, he had almost forgotten what forests and open plains and mountain ranges looked like. The men who'd driven him down here, the little pink ones without hairy pelts, had deserved the deaths he had brought them.

Sometimes, he wondered if he should have left the one who talked too much alive. He couldn't change it now. He had ripped him limb from limb. Eaten his flesh, his brains, his eyes, his guts. But it was so long ago.

Since his last meal of man-flesh, he

had only eaten bats and rats and bugs and the occasional slithering snake venturing too far into the depths of the caverns. Had only drank from the natural run-off filtering through the ground and dripping down the cavern walls into a thin stream, but now, hearing this much industry on the land above, an old bloodlust stirred.

Before the men chased and harried him into his inescapable prison, he had never tasted the flesh of man. He had gone out of his way to avoid them, but once they had surrounded him, firing their stinging weapons, and trying to snare him in their traps, he was forced to kill. As he grew hungrier, he was left with no alternative but to eat, and as it turned out, he liked the taste of their blood, of their flesh.

They were lucky he was trapped here in this place, because if given a choice, he would feast on as many of them as possible, and not solely because he had grown bored of the meagre, bony offerings of the prey he could scrounge in this subterranean pit.

As something howled far above the prison, and the shouting continued, Trog grabbed one of Shackleton's leg bones and beat it against the prison's iron bars as loudly as he could.

CHAPTER FIVE

Beneath his mask, Zombie was smiling as widely as he'd smiled in weeks. No matter the stress he'd been feeling regarding the group seeming to come undone lately, he loved this part of things. The initial shock and awe assault on a property was like foreplay to him. Somewhere inside the house, the girl in there was as frightened as a little rabbit gone to ground while a pack of rabid dogs sniffed its burrow. Before too long, they'd dig her out and have their fun.

Before they did, though, they had to be sure no one else was home. It would only take one little mistake to get themselves in trouble. One little mistake like the one they'd experienced on the outskirts of Katherine in the Northern Territory.

They hadn't checked carefully enough before beginning what they liked to call the roping process. They'd been stringing a young father up, tying his feet at one end, and then tying his hands at the other when an old bloke had burst out of a door and taken a potshot with his shotgun. Thankfully, he'd missed and Skull had plugged him, taking him out of action, but it could have been different. It could have been lethal.

"Go and tell Wolf to remember the process. Before he goes nuts with his chainsaw, we need to secure the hunting ground."

Skull crunched across broken glass in her black Doc Martens boots, heading off to pass the message onto Wolf when a loud, repetitive thudding sound came from somewhere beneath them.

"Wait!" Zombie snapped. "What the fuck is that?"

Skull shrugged her shoulders. "No idea. Some sort of machinery."

It wasn't machinery, it sounded like someone beating a stick on something metallic. Was there a shed here on the property? Did the girl have a brother who played the drums or something?

"Tell me if I'm wrong, but we've only seen one so far, right?"

Skull dropped to her haunches, keeping her head lowered and out of sight of the nearest window. "Yeah, no one else yet."

"Change of plans. You and Wolf check the premises. Make sure there are no parents with shotguns or crossbows, or fucking hunting rifles hiding in any nooks or crannies, and wait for me to get back."

"Where are you going?"

He waited for a fresh bout of knocking

to finish before responding.

"I'm making sure there's no granny-flat or shed or caravan or whatever else these fucking hicks might have on the property where someone could hide."

"And the girl? Want me to make sure Wolf doesn't touch her?"

If there was one thing Zombie appreciated about Skull, it was her intelligence. She was a smart cookie. While he provided the malice, and Wolf delivered hefty helpings of chaos to any siege, it was Skull who brought the brains. She was as sadistic as he was, but she was cunning. Sly. It was sexy. Not that it mattered. She was as uninterested in the pleasures of the flesh as she was in the pleas of her victims when she was free to torture them.

"You know the drill. Keep her stewing in fear before we even attempt to smoke her out of whatever hole she's hiding in."

The beating sound coming from belowground was accompanied by a moaning roar. If he didn't know better, he'd say it was coming from within the earth itself. It must be a trick of the landscape, though. Maybe it was echoing through the ground, off the surrounding hills.

"Get it done. I'm off to find our little drummer boy."

With a quick and simple movement, he leapt off the patio and prowled the walls surrounding the gap between the house and the ground. He loved these old Queenslanders. Back before he'd decided settling down and staying in a single place was a trap, he had wanted to call one home. When he was a kid, some friends of his parents had owned a similar kind of place, and they kept a treasure trove of exciting shit below it. Unlike this one, it was enclosed with a simple wall and concrete floor, and they'd turned it into a paradise of entertainment. They had a pool table down there, table tennis, a few weights, it was everything a young man thought a house needed.

This one was far more primitive. While there was the usual collection of domestic garden tools stacked on a fold-out table, some bikes, and a few other unimportant odds and ends, it was rudimentary. The ground had never been sealed. The house's floorboards were directly visible above it too, an open invitation to pests.

Somewhere on the property, someone was beating an angry tattoo on something, and they had no musical talent whatsoever. If he could locate them, he would be able to devise a plan of attack to ambush whoever was in there. Funnily enough, ambushing people in their own homes was far easier than it should have been.

In stories, homes were presented like fortresses. *A man's home is his castle was bullshit. A man's home is his prison.* With half the youth of today permanently trapped inside their noise-cancelling earphones, the endlessly scrolling screens of technology, and the creature comforts consumer culture thrust upon them, they were sitting ducks, trapped in warrens of rooms, hallways, and furniture. What happened inside those homes was almost unseeable by the naked eye. The four walls of a home did a poor job of keeping people out, but they kept secrets away from prying eyes with great success.

His parents had taken advantage of that when they raised him like an animal, and he'd eventually returned the favour when he had murdered them in their sleep. Several stints in juvenile detention centres, and then more traditional adult detention centres hadn't changed his way of thinking. Doing horrible things to people behind closed doors was nothing but joy for Zombie, and he didn't think it was ever going to change.

Following the angry thumping sound, he ducked under the house's central water pipe, noticing a door in the ground. Freshly cleaned and brushed, there was no way the owners of the house didn't know about it. The fact the beating noise was coming from beyond could mean only one thing: someone was down there.

He squatted over the door and rapped his knuckles on the timber. Seconds later, a huge bellowing roar followed. *What the hell?*

The door didn't budge when he pulled on it. It didn't look like it was locked from the outside, but between the thin crack between the two doors, he could see some sort of bar in place. *Locked from the inside.*

Fuck it. It was a job for Wolf and his chainsaw.

He rapped on the timber again, and the bellowing resumed in response. So did the clanging sound. If there was a kid down there playing drums, he was certainly unique. Still, these weird avant-garde musicians had strange ways. He'd get Wolf and get down there as soon as he could. They couldn't take any chances. All the stress he'd felt between the group lately probably had a lot to do with the feeling they'd gotten away with their murders too easily too many times and trouble had to be on the horizon. It was time to be thorough.

He left the door behind, and was just about to climb onto the patio, when headlights lit up the driveway.

CHAPTER SIX

Aisha could hear two arguing voices outside the master bedroom. One of them, a man's voice, presumably the one in the wolf mask, wanted to cut the door open and drag her out of the room. The other was stopping him. She claimed he knew the rules and until the house was guaranteed to be secure, he'd just have to wait.

For a brief period, she'd thought the third character was under the house. She'd heard him moving around down there when she was about to climb out the window. Not knowing how much of a risk it was, she'd turned her attention to positioning makeshift traps in various places around the room. Until the guy downstairs cleared out, she'd have to hold on. She was certain he'd found the door beneath the house and had knocked on it, because the bellowing she'd been hearing was becoming more and more frequent, and it was getting harder and harder to believe it was just the dripping of water.

She'd emptied Mum's decorative pot-plants and filled them up with bleach. If anyone came through the door, she'd be splashing it in their faces, and she didn't care who you were. Bleach in the face would hurt like a bitch. As she'd positioned the pots near the door, she'd had to think again just how unlucky she had to be for this to be happening and how she had to learn from her experiences with Don Patrickson if she wanted to survive unscathed.

The city was supposed to be the place where things like this occurred. You weren't supposed to move for your 'tree-change' and end up the target of demented home invaders. That was full-blown craziness. The country was supposed to be safer than the city. Everyone said so.

With the bleach-trap in place, she turned her attention to the next step: setting up the fire-zone. She had to be relatively careful with this, given the perfumes and materials in Mum's walk-in, but she'd found a candle lighter and some candles next to the spa bath. With the aerosols and bug-spray available to her, she could scorch the hell out of anyone who tried to approach.

In the corridor outside the room, the two voices stopped. Footsteps moved away from the door, towards the front of the house. What she heard them say filled her with a bizarre mixture of excitement and dread.

"Fucking car!"

Her parents! If these guys hid and ambushed them, they'd have no chance. *She had to warn them, whether the guy was outside or not.*

She scrambled up the toilet and pulled herself out the window. Trying desperately to get out quietly, she dragged her legs through and lowered herself to the ground. She couldn't spot the guy in the zombie mask. The glow of headlights stretched across the front yard and into the dust under the house. He wasn't there.

Heart beating frantically, she ran wide of the house, hiding behind bushes. The car came to a stop and the headlights died. Zombie was still nowhere to be seen, but Wolf and Skull mask were both standing on the patio. Wolf had his chainsaw clutched in both hands. Skull held the sledgehammer.

"Who is that?" her old man asked.

Mum raised her mobile phone. She must have been trying to call.

Aisha gathered all her courage and ran for the car. "Mum! Dad!"

Mum spun her head to look at her just as Zombie appeared on the other side of the car, pointing a gun at Dad.

"FUCKING FREEZE!" Zombie bellowed. "If you want him to live, you'll stay dead still. And trust me, I'll blow him away. He won't be the first!"

Aisha did as he said. With a gun pointed at Dad's head, she had to stop exactly where she was.

"Wolf!" Zombie mask called. "Come and get the kid."

Wolf howled.

Aisha met Mum's eyes as tears welled in her own. Wolf approached, howling all the way.

"Skull, Mum's yours. Grab her."

Skull followed suit, and Zombie mask pulled Dad from the car, never letting the gun drop.

"Who are you?" Dad asked. "Is it money you want? We can pay you."

Zombie pistol-whipped him, leaving him in a heap.

Aisha jerked towards him, but Wolf was already on her. He pinned her arms to her back and dropped her to the ground. As far as she knew, Skull had done similar with Mum.

The bellowing roars from beneath the house continued.

"What the fuck is that?" Wolf hissed in her ear. "You keeping a goddamn Godzilla out here somewhere."

Aisha struggled against his grip.

"No answer. Whatever. We'll make you talk."

Next thing she knew, Aisha was being dragged across the grass by her feet and up the stairs to the patio. She tried as hard as she could to avoid her head clattering into the steps, but Wolf didn't exactly put much care into moving her.

"Sorry," he said. "Not!"

Even if he wasn't a psychotic home invader, everything about him screamed fuckwit: the howling, the over-the-top approach to the invasion, almost like he was trying to be a movie character and not a real person, and especially, his smug attitude. She made a promise to herself: if she got half a chance, she'd kick him in the balls. Hard.

He dragged her into the lounge room and directed her to a chair. "Make yourself at home," he said, chuckling like he'd told the best joke ever. "We won't keep you long."

Moments later, Skull guided Mum into the room and told her to sit beside Aisha. Zombie and her father followed soon after.

Another roaring growl came up from the ground beneath the house.

"Okay, first question," Zombie said, pointing at the floor. "What the fuck have you got hidden in the basement?"

Aisha looked to Dad for an answer. He could only shrug his shoulders. "Sorry, we only moved in just over a week ago. We haven't even looked down there yet. We wanted—"

"Bullshit!" Skull blurted. "Whatever you've got down there has been screaming and hollering since we got here."

"Enough!" Zombie said. He strode across the room and grabbed Aisha by the ponytail, yanking her off the chair and onto her tiptoes. She squirmed and writhed, shoving and kicking at her aggressor, but she couldn't get away. He was holding her too tightly.

Dad leapt to her defence, but Wolf met him with a solid uppercut to the stomach, dropping him straight to his knees. "No heroics."

When Zombie pulled a knife and pressed it to Aisha's throat, she grunted. Froze. This was so much worse than the

Patrickson invasion. He had entered her room in the night, watched her sleep, cut her hair—and God knew what else—but he'd never physically hurt her. He'd still temporarily ruined her life, but he was a pervert, not a psychopath. These guys, they were psychotic to the core, and Aisha feared for her future.

"Now, you will tell me what the fuck is down there, or will I gut your little girl like a fish?"

"Shit, you have to believe me. We haven't even been able to open the door. It's like it's been locked from the inside, and I wanted to get an engineer."

"For fuck's sake," Zombie said, dropping Aisha.

She crawled to Mum and cried into her legs.

"What the fuck?" Wolf asked.

"He's telling the truth. It's locked from the inside."

"So?"

"So, threatening him and killing his girl before we've followed through with our plan doesn't serve any purpose."

Wolf grunted.

"We're going to kill them anyway," Skull said.

Aisha felt a cold chill wash over her.

"No one has to die," Dad said, slowly moving towards Aisha. "If we can get it open, I'll take you down there."

Zombie appeared amused. "You're going to die," he said, "but I'll take you up on your offer." He spun to face Wolf. "You and Dad here, go down to the door. Take the chainsaw. Cut it open. If he tries anything funny, waste him."

Skull coughed politely. "Just a moment," she said. "Are we forgetting our purpose for being here? If it's not been opened, why can't we just get on with our fun and get the fuck out of here? This feels like an unnecessary complication.

"Humour me," Zombie said. "I don't

know what's down there, but if it's not some weird kid with some weird band like I originally thought it was, I want to see what's making all the racket."

CHAPTER SEVEN

Even if the guy in the wolf mask wasn't currently leading Garrett under the house by continually prodding him with the round edge of his unpowered chainsaw, Garret wouldn't trust him one bit. Not only was he quite obviously a dangerous lunatic, but he'd been looking at Aisha like a piece of meat, and Garrett couldn't stand it. No one looked at his daughter like she was meat. Especially some creepy lunatic in a cheap-store werewolf mask. *He couldn't fail her again.* "What do you guys want from us anyway?"

Wolf laughed. "What do we want? Blood. Obviously. You in your house, with your family, thinking you've got it all figured out. Trapped into a mortgage you'll never pay, willingly signing yourself into slavery for what? Big bedrooms? Three toilets? Carpeted floors? Idiot."

"So, you want to kill us because we live in a house. You're unhinged."

Wolf spun on him. "Not really. I want to kill you because it's fun. This isn't a political statement. It's entertainment. Now where's this fucking door?"

Garrett pointed to the depression in the ground.

Wolf adjusted the chainsaw strap and pulled the cord, powering up the tool. "You think this goes straight down?" he asked. "Like, if I stand on it and cut, I'll fall through?"

Garrett truly had no idea, but finding out could be fun and might be a way for this crazy bastard to take himself out. "I hope so."

Wolf spun and held the idling chainsaw in his face. "Zombie said not to kill you. He won't care if I rough you up a bit."

Garrett couldn't help but feel intimidated. There was something about a revving chainsaw that put him on edge. Having grown up on the *Evil Dead* and *Texas Chain Saw Massacre* movies, not to mention the *Doom* videogames, the sound was ingrained in his mind as one associated with violence and great harm. Despite his hackles being up, though, Garrett never saw himself as a wimp.

He'd brought the biff a few times in his life. He was a firm believer that when you were threatened and every other conceivable solution had played out, violence was a necessary option. Considering he'd found out at a Slipknot gig many years ago he had a relatively mean punch on him, he wondered whether he could cold-cock this douchebag. For now, the chainsaw, billowing gas fumes and chugging with latent threat, was enough to stop him from trying it, but if he played his cards right, he might get a chance once they were through the door. This Wolf guy already seemed to have stopped regarding him as a threat. If he waited, he'd get an opportunity.

Refusing to be the first to look away from Wolf's glare, he held Wolf's eyes until the big mask-wearing psycho laughed him off. "Come on, we've got a job to do." He pointed to the other side of the door. "Stand there! Don't move."

Wolf revved the chainsaw, setting the blades in motion and pressed it into the door. Splinters and sawdust fountained up and out as the saw did its work. He started by cutting a long gash adjacent to the top. The cut gouged its way across both doors. He looked up at Garrett and grinned.

Garrett didn't return the expression. He was wondering how he could spin the situation to his benefit. This was also the dumbest possible way to get beyond the door. "Why didn't you just cut the bar locking it from the inside?"

Wolf looked at him, his human eyes confused within the dark recesses of the eyeholes in the mask. Chips of sawdust were stuck in the shaggy fur. Briefly, Garrett wondered why the dude hadn't taken it off to complete the task more easily, but then quickly changed his way of thinking. He'd seen movies. *Seeing this wanker without his mask would be bad news indeed.*

"What do you mean?" Wolf asked.

Garrett pointed at the slit between the two doors. It opened like an old saloon door, and the bar used to lock it was wedged on rungs inside. "See what I mean? Give me the chainsaw and I'll show you."

"Ha! No fucking way! You're not getting credit for this!"

Jesus Christ, he was about as smart as a box of hammers. "Have it your way. I'd definitely cut the bar in the middle, though. It'll save you some work."

Wolf grunted and went back to cutting

the timber his own way.

Garrett watched on. Once upon a time, he'd have been amazed at the wilful stupidity of people when they felt they had to be right, but having worked an office job with other humans for the past twenty years, he'd grown used to it. Stupidity was a part of daily life.

As Wolf continued his third cut, the door started to splinter and fall away on the right-hand side. Miraculously, it balanced, teetering, but not falling.

"What the fuck?" Wolf growled.

Garrett did smile this time. "It's balancing on the crossbar I told you to cut. See: you've cut a big square around it, and while the right-hand side would fall away normally, it's balancing on the crossbar."

"Who's doing this?" Wolf asked and went back to cutting it his way.

Well, at least if there was something horrible down there, there was no way to lock it in again now.

Wolf finished and the entire square collapsed inwards. As it fell, Garrett could have sworn he heard a snarling growl of rage. The wood dropped for what felt like an age before clattering to the bottom of the passage with a huge metallic crash. Dust puffed upward, coating Wolf's mask in fine grey sediment.

Garrett coughed. A howling roar of seething anger tore out of the ground. Whoever had sealed this had done it for what must have been a solid reason.

"What the absolute fuck have you got down here?"

Garrett was wondering the same thing. "I told you. I have no idea, but whatever it is, it sounds pissed."

He knew this part of the country was home to loads of extinct megafauna back in the time of Gondwana, maybe some of it had survived in a deep, dark cave. Hypothetically, at least. Everyone knew about Coelacanth, and the Wollemi Pines found in a gorge in, well, Wollemi.

"You first," Wolf said, pointing. "Ladder looks like it's in good condition."

The ladder did not look like it was in good condition. It was rusted, covered in dust, and ancient. There was no way of telling if it was affixed properly to the wall, and it had not been structurally tested by an engineer. But Wolf had a chainsaw. Garrett had no choice in the matter.

"Are you sure you don't want me to hold the chainsaw so you can go first? I wouldn't want to take any credit for whatever it is you find down there."

Wolf stared dumbly. "Are you serious?"

"Yeah, of course. I mean, how do you know I don't have a shotgun down there. It's possible I know everything about this cavern, and it's only locked from the inside because I have a second entry over the hill there."

Garrett didn't think it was possible, but beyond the eyeholes of the dusty wolf mask, it was obvious Wolf was staring even more dumbly, considering the possibilities. For a split-second, Garrett thought the big dumbass was about to hand over the chainsaw. Wolf's eyes narrowed before it could happen, though.

"I'm gonna take great pleasure in giving you all the chainsaw you could possibly want," he said. "Your wife and daughter too. Oh yeah, they're gonna get the fucking chainsaw all right."

"I'll see you dead, you fucking asshole. I hope you know that."

"Get in the goddamn hole, *Dad*."

Garrett bit back another retort and began his descent.

CHAPTER EIGHT

Humans were coming down the passage for the first time in years. The sounds they made reverberated through the entire passage, vibrating through the walls and being audibly channelled through the open space. Soon, he would eat again.

Skittering bits of debris continued to bounce off the ground and go in all directions. The passage adjacent to the huge cavern of the beast's prison was long and deep. Trog had no idea what else might come down before the humans, but he was eager to watch.

At the mouth of the passage, beams of light began to filter through. The beast knew these were not beams of sunlight. The radiance was wrong, and a creature such as he, so in-tune with the native world, would have recognised sunlight immediately. He had missed the warmth of the sun for decades now, and hoped desperately to one day bask in its glory again.

Suddenly, the squealing, churning noise far above stopped, and there was a splintering sound. Trog felt air rush. And then something huge crashed to the ground with a powerful thud. Dust mushroomed in all directions. He wafted it clear of his face, as voices far above continued.

He inspected the remains of the door closely. Something which clanged like the smooth material of its prison had landed near by. For decades he had tried to use the bones of Shackleton and the other captor as leverage on the door, hoping to pry open the gate, but they had all splintered and turned to powder when he applied pressure.

Amongst the wreckage of the timber doors, he saw exactly what he had hoped for all these years: a thick length of the hard material. And it was within reach.

As the voices continued and lights flashed down the passage, Trog grasped the metal bar and dragged it deep inside the cage. For the first time in ages, he felt hope as well as hunger.

He wedged the length inside the gate, the logical weak point of his prison, and heaved with all his might.

CHAPTER NINE

The sounds coming from below the house had everyone on edge. Aisha leaned into her mother and pretended she was crying, desperate to figure out some kind of escape plan. Since Don Patrickson had forced himself into her life, she'd had to learn resilience. She'd become the subject of his attentions thanks to a media piece about her efforts on the school gym team. It had derailed her for a long time, but thanks to therapy, some extra self-defence classes, and the news Patrickson, an early-thirties computer programmer with subscriptions to all the usual suspects on YOUTUBE, was caught breaking into another girl's house and had been locked up for twelve years, she'd begun to heal. Just when she'd felt confident enough to go back out onto the streets, her parents had decided they were moving. And then this whole thing happened. She couldn't get a break.

If there was one thing she wasn't going to do, though, it was give in and do nothing while these assholes came and ruined her life just as it had gotten better—despite the move out to the bush—and let them conquer and kill her or her family. Before she tried any heroics, though, she needed to convince them she was the weak little girl they probably expected. Then, when she showed them she was actually a superhero, she'd have the element of surprise on her side.

As she kept her face buried in Mum's shoulder, she begged to her to stay watchful and not to give anything away, promised there was a way out, provided they could get these two to drop their guard.

Mum, she knew, was worried about Dad. And why shouldn't she be? They'd heard the chain-sawing, they'd heard the extra bellowing, and they'd heard the crash of something heavy plummeting a long distance, with no sound coming from down there since, they couldn't know whether he was okay or not. Especially with all the extra bellowing coming from deep below the house growing in volume since the crash of the doors.

She knew in her heart there was something beyond the door. Which meant if Dad was going into the cavern, there was a very good chance he'd come face-to-face with it. Whatever it was, it didn't sound friendly. Given there weren't supposed to be any big, land-based predators here in Australia, not for years and years, she knew whatever was making the noise was not something normal and it had the capacity to do serious harm.

Mum was trembling with rage and fear. It was a rational response, but it also meant Aisha had to be the brains here. If they were going to get out alive, they couldn't both lose their minds. It was simple board game logic. She'd played *Elder Sign* with Dad enough times to know mistakes would be fatal and would leave them at the mercy of the Halloween freaks, or the *whatever the hell lived below the house.* "Stay calm, Mum. Stay calm," Aisha whispered, knowing any sudden movements could be fatal.

The two home invaders watching them were clearly scared of whatever was making those sounds also. Both kept looking out the window. They hissed accusations and suggestions to each other, and it was obvious Skull was pissed with Zombie for forcing Wolf to investigate the cave. They'd been fighting about it since Wolf left with Dad, but since the escalation in growling and roaring, things had gotten more intense. She tuned back in to their discussion as the sounds of enraged roaring died to a stop.

"If you were going to make some kinda decision on the fly like this, you needed to run it past us. Six houses. Six houses all ticked off without a glitch apart from one. You know when we hit that glitch? When we veered from the plan!"

"If we don't find out who the fuck is making all the noise, and kill them before we start going Richard Ramirez on this family, then we're asking for trouble. It was locked from inside. Inside, Skull! Do you understand? It means whoever is down there could get out if they wanted to, and they could call the cops, they could take potshots at us, they could get us arrested."

Skull scratched her head with the tip of her knife. "Okay, but then why not back straight out? These people don't know who we are. Their car is out of action. They haven't seen us without the masks. We can just get the fuck out of here and pretend this never happened."

It would have been the smart choice, Aisha thought. *Unfortunately, it was too late.* They had already broken into the passage, and there was no person down there she was aware of, only the thing that screamed and moaned and thumped on the walls. No human could possibly make those noises. Given no one had lived in this beat-up old house for several decades, it was something *real* bad and it had been locked up for a reason.

Zombie brushed glass away from the windowsill and sat down. "This is part of the normal plan. We sweep the premises and make sure there are no stragglers. Why do you have such a problem with it? I do not understand."

"It's probably the demonic noises coming from the pit of hell beneath our house!" Aisha couldn't help herself. She wanted the girl, Skull, to convince this hard-headed fuckface to bail on his plan. To realise there was bad juju in the air and killing was a bad idea tonight.

"Shut your fucking mouth!" Zombie snapped to his feet and raised his gun, ready to pistol-whip Aisha as he strode forward at pace.

Mum didn't give him a chance. In their argument, the freaks must have forgotten they hadn't tied the girls down and had used only the threat of violence to keep them in line. Mum lunged forward, headbutting Zombie straight in the chest and knocking him off balance. He pulled the trigger as he fell, blasting a hole in the ceiling.

The force of Mum's vaulting blow meant she landed on him and was able to clamp her hands down on his wrists, desperate to fight the gun from him.

Under any other circumstances, Aisha would have been impressed. Right now, though, she'd been counting on Mum not doing something like this.

Knowing she had to back Mum up, she was about to kick the gun further away from Zombie when Skull came running over, ready to put the boot in. Aisha jumped in front of her. The two of them fell to the ground, grappling with each other. Aisha drove her fists down into Skull's stupid Halloween mask. They slipped and bounced off the latex, but the weight of her blows had to be doing serious damage. Or so she thought. Somehow, though, Skull, wriggling and writhing, managed to get herself in position and drive a hard knee into Aisha's solar plexus, knocking the wind from her, leaving her gasping for air.

Aisha, fighting through the pain, reached for Skull as she leapt for the gun, but she could only grab a sliding hold on Skull's boot. She tried to yank the woman back, but Skull was too strong, too malicious. She kicked back and the sole of her boot crunched into Aisha's shoulder, knocking her loose. Skull scrambled for the gun.

So did Mum.

In the mad panic, Mum had hold of the weapon for a second, but a firm blow from Zombie's gloved hand made her drop it.

Skull snatched it up, swivelled with it.

BANG!

A spray of blood burst out of Mum's back, splattering around a fresh hole in the wall. The bullet had passed straight through. Mum was turned by the force of the blow. She screamed in agony.

"MUMMMM!" Aisha screamed, diving for her, desperate to see the damage, desperate to make sure Mum was okay, to make sure she was alive. *All of this. The stress, the move, the fucking therapy, just to have Mum yanked away! Goddammit!*

She collapsed onto her yowling Mother, tugging at her dress, searching for the wound. She thought it had gone through her shoulder, but it was lower, lower, somewhere near the bellybutton. *Fuck!*

Rough hands closed on Aisha's throat. She was pulled back and tossed to the floor. Zombie mask stood above her, looking down. The bloody, ripped lips and exposed jawbone of the mask took the place of a snarl. His shoulders heaved with each inhalation and exhalation. Tensions were high, but the dead black eyes of the mask hid Zombie's real expression. For a moment, Aisha thought she glimpsed flat, emotionless eyes. Then, the tuft of braided hair shifted and Zombie drove his boot into her stomach. Again, the wind was knocked out of Aisha.

He kicked her again and again.

She tried to roll away from the blows so she could get to her wailing mum, but the man wouldn't let her past. He had her against the couch, and every time she shifted her weight, he booted her again.

"Stop," she whimpered. "Let me help her."

The man held a gloved finger to the brutalised lips of the zombie mask. "How bad this gets from here is down to you. Do as we say, and we'll make it simple. Keep playing up and we'll make you watch every moment."

Aisha slumped.

"Skull, watch this one."

Skull approached, holding the gun.

Through teary eyes, Aisha stared up at the bitch. With everything she'd been through over the last few years, she thought she'd known hate. Thought she had reserved it only for Patrickson, but no, what she felt there didn't come close to the mix of anger and frustration and desire to harm this evil cow tugging at Aisha's belly and roiling in her guts.

Zombie prowled across to Mum and grabbed her by the hair. "I'm glad you dressed up for tonight," he said, snarling. "Means you'll be dressed appropriately when you get to the pearly gates. Saint Peter will be thrilled."

"Where are you—?"

Skull backhanded Aisha. "You heard him. Shut up," she said. "It's the only way you stop this from getting worse."

It couldn't get worse. Aisha wiped the

82

ZACHARY ASHFORD

blood from her lips. "I'll fucking kill you,"
she said. "You don't know what we've been
through, and I'm not going to have my life
stopped by mask-wearing cowards like
you."

Skull backhanded her again. "You
think this is our first rodeo? You think you
have anything interesting to say? You think
you're the main character who stops our
crimes? Six houses so far, and all of them
thought they were the protagonists of their
own fate, but here's the thing. They were all
NPCs, ready to be executed by faceless
villains like us. Their lives meant nothing.
Neither will yours."

There was no response. Only the
screams of Aisha's mum as Zombie
laughed and tormented her in the guest
bedroom. Below it, the counterpointing
bellows of something terrible grew louder.
Aisha sat back and waited. She needed to
get back on track and think of a plan to
follow through with. Sooner or later, these

morons would make another mistake. If she could be ready for it, she'd be able to act, and hopefully, get to Mum before she bled out.

"Raise your hands," Skull said, pulling heavy zip ties from her tactical belt.

Aisha snorted. "Make me."

Skull stomped on Aisha's bare foot. A jolt of pain shot through the ball of her toe. She reached out to clasp the wounded tissue, but Skull was faster.

She grabbed Aisha by the throat. "You're a tough little bitch, but you're beaten here. You need to deal with it, or this is going to go really hard on you."

Aisha snapped her good foot up, kicking Skull right between the legs. She lunged forward, trying to steal the gun away from her captor, but it was no good. She had just closed a hand around it when Skull kneed her hard in the face. Aisha's vision swam.

Skull was on her, efficiently slapping

her hands back against the bookshelf, looping the first zip tie through the decorated timber design and Aisha's wrist. She yanked it tight and quickly followed with the second hand. She didn't take any chances, looping several more ties around different holes in the shelf and fastening them tight.

Momentarily defeated, Aisha let her head drop. She had the mistake she needed. She knew how weak this bookshelf was. She'd broken many parts of it over the years. She just had to keep it secret a little longer. She satisfied herself with the knowledge Mum's screams were proof of life, and sooner or later, Skull would lose focus.

Until then, she could only hope whatever the hell was below the house didn't make it up here before she was free. Its continued bellowing was a promise. When it made its way out of the ground, it was going to be pissed.

CHAPTER TEN

Edging through the passage, using his flashlight to inspect the rungs of the ladder for trip hazards, Garrett was becoming more and more concerned with the sounds coming from the dark patch of shadow at the base of the passage. Whatever was down here, it was obviously huge. The musty smell of ancient animal urine wafted up from the base of the cavern, and the snarling and grunting he could hear was enough to make his blood run cold. He was sure he could hear the clang of metal on metal. Something breathing heavily.

He looked up the ladder, seeing red wolfen eyes peering at him from behind a long snout. It was impossible to get a read on the man beneath the mask, but he had to be hearing the same thing Garrett was. "I don't think we should go any farther,"

Garrett said, hoping the dude would see sense.

"Keep going," Wolf said, lifting the chainsaw high enough to show he still meant business.

Garrett was a pragmatic man. He didn't take unnecessary risks. He stopped at amber traffic lights no matter how much he thought he could make it through before they turned red. He had never tried chemical drugs for the sole reason he didn't know what was in them, and he never experimented with restaurant meals beyond steak and chips, Bolognese, or pizza. Risks might come with rewards, but they also came with disappointment. It was why they were called risks.

Right now, trapped in what he figured was the biggest risk he had ever taken, he was contemplating trying for one, even more potentially fraught, calculated risk which might help him out of trouble. He locked his left arm around the closest rung and wove it through the exterior frame of the ladder as best he could. "Hold up," he said, "I think there's a broken rung here."

"Go past it, you little pussy."

"Can you lean out and see it?"

Wolf growled, annoyed, and leaned out.

Garrett grabbed Wolf's pants leg and yanked as hard as he could. Unfortunately, his efforts had no effect whatsoever. Wolf shook his leg free. "Nice try," he said. "You think I didn't see it coming a mile away?"

He kicked down, stomping Garrett's shoulder.

Garrett slipped, nearly fell. Managed to hold on thanks to the grip he'd secured only moments earlier.

"Which one of us has the high ground?" Wolf asked. "Dumbass."

A bellowing scream responded before Garrett could.

"Come on, mate," Wolf said, stepping down another rung. "The big scary whatever is waiting for us. Keep moving."

Furious, Garrett continued climbing, hoping like hell there was some sort of escape route once he reached the ground. He'd never be able to shake Wolf down, but if there were passageways he could flee into, objects he could use as weapons, dark crannies in which he could hide, he might be able to fight his way up to his family.

A gunshot rang out far above them. He snapped his head up. Wolf was looking towards it too. Abruptly, he jerked his head back to Garrett. "Didn't sound good."

There was screaming. Another gunshot. A howl of anguish.

"Definitely not—" Wolf began to say.

A loud roar, the loudest yet thundered towards them, channelled by the natural amplification of the tunnel. Garrett's blood froze in his veins. Whatever it was, the creature, for he was certain it was a creature, was incredibly angry. Probably violent. Probably lethal. "Please, mate," he said. "We've got to get back up there. Whatever this is, it's beyond us."

"Beyond you, maybe. Only thing up there for you is death. More gunshots. At least down here, you might be surprised."

Garrett took a deep breath. Fuck this guy. One opportunity was all he'd need to kill him. One opportunity.

He stepped off the ladder and spun to face the tunnel ahead, whipping his torch around, just in case the thing making all the noise was as close as it had sounded.

It was, and it looked as shocked as Garrett.

He didn't know what to make of it. Imprisoned in a cage it was desperate to escape, the biggest fucking creature Garrett had ever seen froze, momentarily halting its heaving on the iron bar it was using to lever open the gate of its prison. It snarled at Garrett. Stared with eyes that flashed in the light of his torch. One word from Garrett's youth came to mind: *Yowie.*

In the artificial light, the monster cast a huge shadow on the back wall of the large cavern which must have held it prisoner for decades. A thick Cro-Magnon brow jutted heavily above black, intelligent, eyes. Its fur, patchy and mange-ridden, was marred by matted spots, mould, and what looked like weeping sores. Above it, on an ancient painted hoarding was a name: TROG THE ANTIPODEAN SASQUATCH.

Holy shit.

Trog watched Garrett as he inspected its sheer size, and then, growing bored, he roared. The creature's mouth was like something from a nightmare. Protruding teeth the size of Garrett's index finger stuck out of both jaws. Four in particular revealed the truth about his diet. This thing was first and foremost a predator. Rows of smaller, but no less jagged, teeth filled the gaps.

"Go up!" Garrett called to Wolf. "Go back up now!"

"What is it?"

The beast heaved on its iron bar again. Its muscles rippled as it grunted.

Something in the gate snapped. The gate flew open and rebounded. The creature bellowed and slammed the gate back on its hinges with a huge palm and leapt for Garrett.

Garrett threw himself sideways, not caring if he fell, as the monster came straight for him. He felt the rush of wind left in its wake. Smelled the must of its mouldy fur. Thankfully, it ignored him as it bolted. It took the rungs of the ladder with the grace of a jungle-dwelling primate, leaping them three, four steps at a time.

Wolf started to scream.

Garrett could only watch the monster grab him as it vaulted up the ladder. Trog took several more steps, pounding Wolf's back against the cavern wall as he climbed. Then, as abruptly as he had fled the cage and grabbed Wolf, he roared, and let the mask-wearing maniac fall.

Wolf crashed to the ground with a pained thud. A cloud of dust erupted around him.

He twitched. Chewed.

Garrett inspected him. Felt his pulse. It was there, but he seemed badly hurt. For a second, Garrett wondered if he should put him out of his misery, but despite his better judgement, he knew he would never be able to sleep again. Besides, he needed to get up to his family. He needed to know those gunshots weren't aimed at Gemma or Aisha.

He took one last look at the board advertising the creature's name. Everyone knew there were no bigfoots, yetis, or sasquatches in Australia. Instead, there were yowies, and there were even Cadbury chocolates named after them. Still, he couldn't help but wonder how long the creature had been trapped down here, presumably by Roger Shackleton, the entrepreneur and conman who'd given the town its name. It was known he was getting a travelling freakshow together to rival the PT Barnum & Bailey Circus of the Americas. He'd obviously captured a yowie, and hoping to make advertising his find to the primarily British audience of the time easier, had referred to it as the Antipodean Sasquatch. As Garrett flashed his torch around the prison, he saw several piles of human bones. *Was this where he had disappeared? Had he locked himself in and been taken by surprise?* It seemed like madness, but Garrett could conceive of no other turn of events capable of leading to this.

Shaking his head, wondering how the beast had managed to survive so long in the darkness, he moved to the base of the ladder. Wolf was down, hopefully for good, but Garrett couldn't be bothered removing the man's mask. Instead, he picked up the chainsaw, looped the strap over his shoulder and, hoping the monster had cleared out and gone straight for the forest, he began his ascent.

As he climbed, one more thought came to him: How long would they have lived above Trog before they found him?

CHAPTER ELEVEN

Zombie hovered over the prone woman. Fuck he hated their stupid 'no killing unless everyone was present' rule. Here, now, this was an obvious moment to put the bitch out of her misery. First, she deserved it. Taking him by surprise had been a dumbass move. Second, she was getting blood everywhere, and she wouldn't stop her damn caterwauling. Finally, he knew Wolf would want more from her than just blood. Zombie hated him for it. It was cheap and nasty, and it always led to arguments. He and Skull had explained to the idiot enough times he couldn't leave evidence of himself behind, but if they didn't keep a close watch on him, he would find a way to get his jollies off.

Zombie figured if he found the death and destruction so exciting, he should be a damn professional and sort himself out when he got home. It was how Zombie managed himself. Skull, he had no idea. He didn't think she ever considered pleasure.

As he watched the bleeding woman try to talk through her duct tape gag, another humongous scream of animal rage boomed below the house. A metallic jarring sound burst out after it, like a gunshot, and the sound of screaming followed. *Wolf?* Abruptly, the sound came to a complete stop. *Can't be good.*

The woman, still wearing the dress she'd worn to whatever engagement had taken them out earlier, was terrified. Her eyes were dilated to the size of saucers.

"You truly don't know what's making that noise, do you?"

She shook her head.

"Let's try this another way, because I

think you do." He stalked across to her and pressed two fingers inside the bullet-wound in her gut. Twisted them around like he was looking for something. The pulpy flesh slipped and moved beneath his fingers. The copper-smell of blood plumed up with each squelching movement of his hand. Tears welled in the woman's eyes.

"Now, either your husband has been keeping secrets, or you know exactly what kind of thing is down there, and I gotta tell you, I'm getting pretty fucking curious, because we've done this a few times now, and nothing as exciting as this has ever happened."

She screamed in agony. Shook her head.

A low growl erupted beneath the house. It sounded like the churning chug of a powerful engine.

Zombie pulled the Glock from his jacket pocket.

"Do you think that's hubby? Or the big

bad monster?"

He located roughly where he thought the growl was emanating from and pulled the trigger, blasting a hole in the floorboards.

In response, something powerful pummelled the floor from beneath him, shaking the whole room.

He took another shot.

This time, there was a yelp of pain. Another thud. A splintering sound.

A huge, primitive hand covered in mangy black fur burst through the floorboards and clamped onto Zombie's ankle. *What the fuck?*

He levelled the Glock. Fired again. Another yelp and the hand disappeared.

The bedroom door burst open, and Skull stuck her head in. "What the hell is going on?"

"There's something fucking huge down there."

"Bullshit!"

Another roar erupted, and this time, the

beast smashed its upper body through the floorboards. Timber splintered and snapped as it swiped at Zombie.

"Get the fuck out of here!" he screamed at Skull. He ran for the door. He'd shot it at least once, and it was still coming. It was time to ditch the scene.

Skull took another look at the thing clambering through the floorboards and levelled her own gun.

The beast disappeared, dropping back beneath sight.

Zombie didn't waste any time. He blasted the floor, hoping a stray round might catch the monster somewhere vital. Skull followed suit.

On the bed, the woman screamed.

The young girl was screaming also.

"Go and see where the fuck Wolf is!"

The beast's hands smashed through the floorboards again. This time it grabbed both of Zombie's ankles and tugged down, pulling him halfway through. His gun went flying underneath the bed.

Skull bolted.

"Let go of me, you fuck!" Zombie shouted. He kicked his feet, hitting something as sturdy and powerful as a mountain of muscle. Then, he felt great pressure on his ribcage. The monster was tugging on him, desperate to pull him clean through the flooring. With a splintering crack, he felt his ribcage collapse as the pressure became too much. Agony swelled in his chest. He screamed in pain.

There was a thudding sound, and then he felt the earth rise up to knock the wind out of him.

Next thing he knew, he was looking at the beast from the ground. It was truly hideous. Its teeth, jagged and pointed and full of rot, dripped with foaming saliva. Its eyes were deeply intelligent, but it didn't take a genius to realise the monster, some sort of bigfoot, was possessed with insane rage.

It screamed in his face.

The last thing he saw was the beast reaching for him.

CHAPTER TWELVE

Garrett, too terrified to risk running past the monster, could only watch in awe as it pulled the dude in the zombie mask through the floor. The sound of screams, and not only Gemma's and Aisha's washed out of the house, but they were drowned by the roaring of Trog.

He'd seen the yowie recoil when the gunshots were being fired, forcing him to duck further into the passage. He'd then heard footsteps bolting across the house and Aisha call out something to the runner, who must have been the bitch in the skull mask. Right now, he was certain the chick was trying to make a break for it. Good luck to her. If it meant his family could live, then

good. And then he realised they'd slashed
his tires. If she took the remaining vehicle,
he'd not be able to get his own family away
from here.

Fuck!

The beast, very obviously male, was
occupied with zombie mask, but Garrett
couldn't make his legs work. Shaking and
sweating and clammy, he pulled himself up.
The chainsaw clattered into the wall of the
cavern and the monster swung its massive
head to see what had made the sound.

Garrett dropped a couple of rungs. Held
his breath. Heard Skull swear from the front
of the house. "Zombie!" she screamed.
"Wolf! Where are the fucking keys?"

Chancing his luck, Garrett looked back at
the beast just in time to see it raise Zombie up
by his throat. Trog shook his captive, who
kicked feebly. He roared in Zombie's face
and then jammed a thumb in what should
be the mouth-hole of the mask. Meeting
only latex, he grunted then tore the mask

free, discarding it without a second thought.

He tried again, jamming three fingers into Zombie's mouth, choking him, and then began to pull up as if prying off the top of a coconut. In an explosion of blood and viscera, the top of the dude's head snapped free, leaving only a wagging tongue and the top of a spinal cord attached to his body. The monster dropped its kill and Zombie's eyeballs slipped out of the half-skull left in Trog's hand. He fished the brains out and slurped them from his massive palm.

Holy shit.

The monster looked around, then climbed back through the hole in the floorboards.

Gemma started screaming again. Aisha soon followed.

Garrett knew he'd need to find those car keys, but first, he had to make sure his girls were okay. If they had to walk out of here, they would, but neither Gemma nor Aisha could wait for him any longer.

He bolted towards the veranda, and the front door.

CHAPTER THIRTEEN

Frustrated with her inability to know exactly what was going on in her whimpering mum's room, Aisha tugged hard on the zip ties fastening her to the bookshelf. She'd first broken parts of it back when she was barely in double digits. She'd been trying to climb up to one of the top shelves and grab a really interesting-looking book with a super colourful cover Dad had shown her before filing it beyond her reach. From memory, she thought it was some old horror book about vampires in Los Angeles. She couldn't be sure now, but she thought it was a McCammon.

Now, ignoring the pain the zip ties caused as she applied pressure and they cut into her skin, she could remember how it had happened. She'd tried to use the shelf like a ladder. Thankfully, Granddad had followed the proper instructions and secured it to the wall, because she hated to think what might have happened if he hadn't. As it was, she'd broken one of the shelves and she'd slipped to the ground, books tumbling all over her.

The timber creaked as shouts rang out from the spare bedroom and loud growling erupted from beneath the house. Then the gunshots had started, the crashing and tearing sounds, and Skull had sprinted past her, leaving the house as quickly as she could. Then, as slurping and roaring beneath the house had provided the backdrop, Skull had bellowed something about keys. The crazy bitch was undoubtedly going to head back into the house any time now in a desperate search for them, and Aisha wanted to be free beforehand, especially as she could now hear something huge breaking things in the room, and her mum screaming.

"I'm coming, Mum!"

Footsteps on the patio made her think Skull had come back already, then Dad stuck his head into the room, shushing her. "Thank God!" she said. "They shot Mum!"

"You've got to be quiet," Dad said, rushing across to her, and tugged on the ties. When they didn't come immediately, he leaned across to the drawer under the television and pulled out a Stanley knife. He cut the ties as quickly as he could. "Where's your mum?"

"Spare room."

Dad's eyes clouded. His face grew severe. He didn't need to say anything.

"What is it?" Aisha asked, not sure what she should be picturing. Some sort of tentacled monster, some sort of giant mammal, or some sort of bizarre supernatural creature.

"It doesn't matter what it is?"

"Bullshit," Aisha snapped. "Tell me."

"Yowie."

She stared at him, incredulous. As he sliced the last tie, she saw he was serious. No way. A yowie? *They couldn't exist. Surely?*

"You're telling the truth?"

Something big clattered to the floor in the spare room and Mum screamed for help.

Dad stared at the door to the room. Looked at his chainsaw. "I've got to tell you, Aisha. I don't know if I can help your Mum. I saw what it did to that zombie guy, and if it's got her, we can't do anything about it."

There was no way Aisha could accept that. Dad cut the last zip tie, and she got to her feet. Inside the spare room, Mum howled for help, screaming for the thing to, "Get away!"

Her screams were stifled, and Dad shook his head as Aisha edged closer to the door.

Aisha knew her Dad had taken the Patrickson part of her life almost as hard as she had. He'd been working away from home and blamed himself for her vulnerability. If they were forced to leave Mum behind, he'd never recover. "We can't abandon her."

Another scream sounded.

Dad sidled up beside her. "Open the door a crack."

Aisha levered the door handle as quietly as she could and slowly creaked the door open.

The huge hairy thing beyond the door stopped its movements. Cocked an ear in their direction. Snarled. *Holy shit, Dad was telling the truth.* A yowie had hold of Mum. Her face was as white as a sheet. Beads of sweat trickled down her forehead and into her crow's feet. While her mouth was moving, she was in a deep state of shock; almost catatonic. She was cradled in its arms, and its head was lowered to her belly. The monster slurped and grunted with satisfaction. Mum's pleading eyes rolled across to them. Her lips quivered.

"What do we do?" Aisha whispered.

Dad inspected the chainsaw then turned his attention back to the missing link currently holding Mum in a precarious position.

"Maybe it wants to heal her? I've heard they're spiritual creatures."

"It's eating her!" Aisha snarled. She slammed the door open and bolted into the room. "Leave her alone!" she shouted, whacking it repeatedly with two hands.

The beast spun, turning its head with a mouthful of bloody tendons and torn skin. A gibbet of Mum's flesh protruded from between its lips. Holding her by the legs, it whipped her around like a club. A stray intestine unspooled, still caught in the beast's mouth, but it didn't slow her down. Her head smashed into Aisha's midriff, sending her flying back out the door in a crumpled heap.

Aisha pulled herself to her knees as Dad tried to help her to her feet. She stopped mid-movement, unable to look away.

The beast snapped Mum back around, crunching her head on the splintered floorboards where it had entered. Mum's skull cracked. Brains and gore splattered. Blood leaked out of her ears.

As Aisha gawped, feeling her guts sink, the beast screamed and plunged a hand into the huge wound in Mum's belly. It ripped the hand back out, bringing entrails and intestines with it, then threw them at Aisha and roared.

Aisha cried out, but Dad didn't waste any time. Throwing an arm around her waist and lifting, he hefted her up and ran for the front door.

She kicked and screamed, hoping beyond hope she could get Mum out of the room. Hoping she could drag her to safety. Even if she was already dead, she shouldn't be desecrated. She should be buried. She should be prayed over. She should be given a final farewell. If they left her, that thing would consume her and, eventually, Mum would receive the worst insult: to be reduced to prey and shat out on a forest floor somewhere, her life meaningless, just as Skull had said.

"We can't leave her! We can't leave her!"

"It's okay. It's okay. We've just got to get you to safety. Once you're safe, I'll come back for her." As he passed, Dad yanked the spare car key so hard from its hook the whole thing clattered off the wall. When he reached the front veranda, he dropped Aisha to her feet, but he didn't stop running, dragging her by the wrist.

Even following, Aisha couldn't help but look over her shoulder, watching the rapidly diminishing veranda for signs the beast was following. So far, the creature had remained behind. She didn't want to think about what it could be doing in there.

Aisha saw the damage done to the car before he did, but he wasn't far behind.

While she was looking at the wickedly slashed tyres, he was busy swearing at the cut wires protruding from the fuse box.

She turned her attention back to the house, gauging how much time they had. In the dim light, Skull was emerging from the storage area.

She still had a gun, but something else caught Aisha's attention. She was also carrying something which glinted in the moonlight. Keys.

"Dad!" Aisha said. Skull mask was coming.

CHAPTER FOURTEEN

Trog raised his head from the wound in the woman's belly and licked blood from his lips. It had been so long since he had feasted on anything meaningful, the simple of act of burying his face in a fresh kill and chewing out the guts and organs gave him

ZACHARY ASHFORD

pleasure beyond imagining.

There were still other humans here, but right now, he was so busy filling his belly, feeling nutrients flow through his system he could barely consider what he would do with the humans if he caught them. It wasn't like he could kill and eat them all in one night.

But…

…the place he had been kept might serve well if he could secure it again. In his youth, he had been nomadic, wandering the forests with a clan, a tribe of long-lived beings at one with nature. They had hunted for meat when necessary and picked ripe fruits when they felt like it, but it had been so long since he had seen the forest, he wasn't exactly sure life would be easy back amongst the trees. A ready supply of humans, trapped and unable to escape, might be exactly the kind of thing allowing him to explore the forest on his own terms. He could even use this place as a home while he figured out how much had changed, where his family was, what he would do to survive going forward.

He bit down on one of the woman's fingers, letting sharp teeth press against bone, and then peeled the flesh and skin back with his teeth, much like a person would eat a chicken wing. He gulped the meat down and gave chase.

The humans would not have gotten far, but if he left them too much time, they might split up and make hunting them harder. He went through the door the other two humans had appeared in and followed their scent out the front.

CHAPTER FIFTEEN

The waves of sickness had stuck with Skull since she'd seen the state of Zombie's head. She fought them down as she squatted low, inspecting the lay of the land before venturing into the front yard. She didn't think the beast was close enough to act immediately, but she didn't want to take any chances. Zombie's head had been ripped in half, the eyes hanging loose where the socket had been pulled from and the sinew had stretched and warped as the cartilage and bone had ripped. The skin around the corners of the mouth had been torn like taffy. The crown of the skull had been scooped clean of brains and left upside-down on the ground like a discarded bowl. She did not want the same thing to happen to her.

Edging forward, trying not to be seen by the father and his tough bitch of a daughter, she surveyed the front yard. Despite them hovering around their destroyed car, she couldn't stop to worry about them. She'd have to run past them and hope they didn't stop her. For what might have been the first time in her life, a pang of guilt—a minor pang, but a pang nonetheless—let itself be known.

It had been her who'd devised the idea to eliminate obvious escape routes when they invaded a property, and slashing tyres, cutting wires, and puncturing petrol tanks was a quick and easy way to remove the potential escape avenue offered by a vehicle. They'd set to work on that within seconds of taking the family captive. Now, with things having gone awry and having full knowledge of the damage the cryptid could do, she had to wonder if such an act was stupid. What if she needed their car to escape? What if she's forced to make a break for it because Wolf or Zombie had fled in their own car. She'd be screwed. Zombie's brutalised body was enough proof she didn't want to come face to face with the fucking sasquatch-thing again. Wolf's disappearance meant the beast had either killed him already or he had bailed like a coward as soon as he'd seen it. Both were highly possible.

She had been just about done with this shit when they finished the last house, and now, all she wanted was to leave the country. Tensions had been growing between Wolf and Zombie for a few days, and she was sick of the bickering. She wanted to find a nice, quiet, backwoods town somewhere on the other side of the world and blend into the local community there, never speaking of what she'd done over the last few months.

When she'd first got involved, she'd loved it. It had been a great way to hurt people and get away with it free of consequences. She'd found the others on a 4Chan forum after being drawn to their hateful view of the world. She had been told on many occasions she was a sociopath, and on an intrinsic level, she accepted it. What she liked about her conversations with Zombie and Wolf, though, wasn't just their hatred, but the fact it was geared towards everyone they deemed responsible for the modern way of life. Hating someone because of their race or religion was a ridiculous notion which would never bring change to the world in a meaningful way. Sure, a race-war was a possibility, but for her, targeting the family unit, those who were so happy and comfortable in capitalist society was a far better way to vent her frustrations. She hated the way everyone was stuck to their screens and plugged into their self-moderated newsfeeds while shadow governments and corporations rode them into the ground. *Sheeple, the lot of them.*

She had lived homeless for years, only getting off the streets thanks to her ability to commit crimes without her conscience getting involved. If she could lash out and hurt those who sat comfortably on plush couches, she could claim a little bit of the control she had never had in her younger life.

But tonight's events sent all her plans

to the big fiery pit in the ground; she had attended one raid too many. She should have listened to her gut and called it quits earlier in the week. Now, with the appearance of a literal creature of myth and legend coming to end their run of violent home invasions with a little brutality of its own, she'd promise to never commit another crime again if she could make it out alive. Comeuppance like this had its own special brand of permanence.

Satisfied the coast was as clear as it was going to get, and certain the beast was still inside the house, she took her opportunity to make a break for Zombie's Ford station wagon.

"She's got keys!" the girl said as Skull sprinted past her. Skull ignored her and kept sprinting.

"Aisha, no!" Dad yelled.

Skull couldn't ignore it. She turned on her heels just in time to see the girl closing in on her. She raised her gun, but she was too shocked, too slow to do anything effective with it. The girl took to the air, crunching Skull with a perfect tackle.

CHAPTER SIXTEEN

When Aisha had been stuck at home, moping around the house, terrified to venture outside, she had learned survival wasn't only about staying alive. True survival, the kind that saw everything about the life you loved continue to thrive couldn't be achieved through passive resistance. Instead, thanks to many discussions with her counsellor, the shelves of heroic YA fiction in her room, and her own willingness to overcome the circumstances she'd found herself in, she had come forward at Patrickson's hearing and shared her story. That moment of active resistance, of willingness to put a stop to his antics, helped convince the jury of his guilt, and had taught her only action could free her from the prison of her mind. That's why she ignored Dad's pleas to stop chasing Skull mask.

This bitch was just as much of an offender as Patrickson, and if they let her get away with the vehicle, happy she'd let them live, it would never be enough to guarantee their own freedom.

Sprinting hard, she dropped her head, dropped her shoulder, and launched herself at Skull's legs. She'd learned to tackle by listening to Dad talk rugby with his mates. She'd never tried it, but the logic seemed simple enough: hit people where they had the least centre of balance.

The impact rocked Skull, driving her to the ground. The gun tumbled across the grass, well out of reach, but Aisha wasn't interested in the weapon at all. She drove her fists down into Skull's mask again and again, harder and harder with every punch.

She remembered how her fists had seemed to bounce off the latex last time, so with each driving punch, she focused her energy on punching through the bone white latex, throwing her weight behind her knuckles and willing Skull's real bones to crack. "Give me the keys, bitch! Give me the fucking keys!" she screamed, making herself hoarse with the anger she felt flowing through her vocal cords.

This time, she didn't give Skull the opportunity to wriggle free, keeping her legs planted firmly on either side. Skull grasped the keys tight in a closed fist as she tried to block the deluge of blows with her forearms.

Aisha grabbed the hand and tried to pry the grip wide, but Skull wasn't going to relinquish them easily. A trickle of blood ran out of her mask like water and Aisha pummelled her again before grabbing the hand holding the keys, trying to slap it on the ground.

"Aisha, move!"

She realised Dad had been hollering at her for a while and he had hold of the gun. He pointed it at Skull.

"Move out of the way!"

As Aisha cleared the path for Dad to take charge, Skull wriggled, throwing her legs and twisting to the side, trying to manoeuvre into a better position to defend herself, but he planted a firm boot in her ribs, spinning her onto her back.

"The keys!"

"Fuck you," Skull whimpered.

"Now!" Dad said, stepping with her as she rolled.

Aisha, unable to tolerate this bitch any further punched her again and grabbed the stupid skeleton mask with both hands. She ripped it clear of the woman's face and gasped.

Skull was far younger than Aisha had expected. She had cropped her hair short, leaving only one braid dangling like a rat's tail, but her face, even beyond the bruises and lacerations from Aisha's recriminations bore several years' worth of scars. The side of her mouth had once been ripped open if the scar stretching from the corner of her lips to her cheek was any evidence. Her eyebrows were shaved in the middles. Her eyes were cold and desperate.

"Aisha," Dad said. "Get out of the way."

She drove another punch into Skull's unmasked face. Her lips mashed against her teeth and burst.

Skull laughed, bubbling blood.

"You can have the keys," she said. "For Christ's sake." She held them out in an open palm. Just as Aisha was about to grab them, Skull snatched her fist closed again and lobbed them into the bushes beyond the car.

"Fucking bitch!" Aisha screamed, hitting her again.

Skull said something back, but Aisha

didn't hear it. The beast had let loose with a terrifying roar.

It stood on the veranda, beating its chest with one meaty palm and waving Mum's severed head around with another. Mum's blood-soaked hair flopped back and forth, spraying droplets of blood across the walls.

Aisha's stomach lurched. *Good God! Mum!*

"Aisha," Dad said. "Get in the car. Now!"

The beast roared again. It leapt clear of the veranda, landing on the grass with a powerful thud, dong bouncing, confirming the beast's sex.

Aisha backed away from Skull, mindful of her ability to kick out and started to move towards the car. "She's all yours!" Aisha shouted at the beast.

"In the car!" Dad growled as he rummaged around the bushes looking for the car keys.

Skull, though, had other ideas. She latched onto Aisha's ankle and tugged. "You're not going anywhere!" She used Aisha's resistance to pull herself closer, then managed to grab Aisha's other foot. She threw her weight into her movements and dragged Aisha to the ground.

"No!" Dad ran closer with the gun pointed at Skull. "Get off her! Get off her!"

Skull laughed.

Aisha howled, throwing punches, and writhing frantically. She'd lost sight of the beast. Worse, Skull had tucked in tight to her, was trying to bite her throat. *She was an animal!*

Aisha turned her head in her attempt to get away and Skull latched onto her left ear with her powerful incisors. She bit down.

Overwhelming pain exploded in Aisha as Skull snarled and tore at her ear with ripping motions of her head.

Dad, unable to take the shot, pistol-whipped Skull, knocking her off Aisha and dragging her to her feet before she could tear any flesh away.

The beast stalked closer, one eye on the gun, another on the commotion. He howled, cocking the arm holding Mum's severed head back like a pistol and then pitched it forward like a fastball. Mum's head whistled through the air, spinning, leaking blood as it traversed the distance in a flat line. The beast's aim was true.

Mum's severed head smashed into the bridge of Dad's nose with a crack so audible it sounded like a gavel falling. Dad's head rocked back, spewing blood. Teeth fell where he stood. He staggered and dropped to the ground, his body convulsing.

Aisha screamed. This couldn't be happening!

Skull was laughing like it was the funniest thing she'd ever seen.

Unable to do more than try to drag Dad to his feet, quickly realising she couldn't lift his dead weight, Aisha scrambled for the gun. It had fallen nearby. She snatched it up and spun on Skull. *If I can get a shot away before the beast gets too close, I can—*

She was too slow. The beast rushed forward and lifted Skull from the ground like a ragdoll. One hand around her chest, another around her waist.

Skull's laughter became screams of agony.

The beast growled and grunted and pulled with considerable might. Skull's body began to stretch. There was a crunching sound, not unlike dry spaghetti snapping, and Aisha realised Skull's spine had torn. Seconds later, blood gushed out of her midsection, and the creature ripped her in half.

A foul stench hit the air, and intestines spilled over the beast. He turned his face upwards and lashed his tongue across the falling ruins of Skull's guts.

Aisha dragged Dad towards the back of

the car, knowing if she couldn't get the thing started, she was doomed. There was no way she could outrun the monster, let alone escape with her father in tow. "Hide here. I'll be right back."

Dad, slowly returning to his senses, pointed. The keys were glistening in the moonlight, resting beside a thicket of brambles. "Unlock it."

She knew he was a tough bastard, but the fact he'd survived a blow of such magnitude was incomprehensible. She snatched up the keys and unlocked the station wagon.

When the locks clicked, she feared the worst, but the beast didn't move. He had cast Skull's legs aside and was busy chewing out the soft contents of her opened stomach. She held the door for Dad, who clambered awkwardly into the back seat.

Aisha, still holding the gun, not sure how to fire it, held it on the beast as she followed Dad in and climbed through the gap between the two front seats. *Thank God the car's an automatic.*

After she'd become a target for Patrickson, Dad had insisted she learn to drive the family car, just in case she ever needed it. *Well, now she needed it.*

"Trog," Dad said as she slipped the key into the ignition.

The monster was watching her, but he still hadn't finished his meal. One crazed eye settled on her face. She wondered if he could smell her fear, whether she was giving off pheromones or chemicals allowing him to know exactly what she was feeling.

"Trog," Dad said again. "Its name is Trog."

What the fuck? Wincing, she turned the key, and the engine stuttered to life. The monster kept chewing, kept watching. What he made of the engine, she had no idea. Slowly, Trog lowered Skull's torso from his face, and still not taking his eye from Aisha, reached into the sleeve of her stomach. Skull's chest rippled and bulged. The monster ripped his hand out, bringing something fleshy with it: Skull's heart. It grinned, popped the organ into its bloody mouth and chewed slowly.

"Shackleton had him imprisoned behind the door," Dad said. "He's starving. Been trapped down there for decades. There are human remains down there. I think he killed Shackleton. That's why he disappeared."

She had no time for a history lesson, but as she dropped the handbrake and slipped the car into gear, she had to ask. "You know its name?"

"There was an advertising hoarding down there. He wanted it for the freakshow."

Trog was a freak all right, a huge, murderous one, and he was still looking Aisha dead in the eye. *So far,* she thought, *it's been all your way, Trog.* She knew she couldn't pull a three-point-turn and get away, so she took the next best option. She planted her foot. *Let's see how you like this, you big hairy motherfucker!*

The car lunged forward, speeding over Skull's discarded legs and crashed into the beast, sending him flying. He rolled, finishing in what looked like a painful heap, then lay still.

Aisha didn't stop. She continued to accelerate, veering the car around the house and spinning through the backyard and out the other side. *Thank fuck for acreage properties and their lack of fences.*

As she sped around the side of the house where the door to Trog's prison had remained unmolested for years, she noticed the big ugly bastard was no longer crumpled in a heap where she'd left him.

Then a crunching thud rang out from the roof of the car. Dented imprints in the shape of gigantic feet pressed down. She screamed, rocking the car from side to side, trying to throw the yowie off the roof, but it was no good. He had a firm grip, and he was stomping down with all his strength.

The car hit the gravel driveway, and Aisha had no choice but to keep accelerating, hoping the vehicle wouldn't skid and hit a tree. This only forced Trog to redouble his efforts.

The sound of tearing metal ripped out from the roof of the car, and a ginormous hairy foot pushed through. The material ceiling cover gaped around it, and the beast stomped down.

Dad narrowly avoided the foot, then threw himself into the open boot of the vehicle.

Aisha couldn't help but turn to see the damage. It was a massive mistake. It only took a split-second without paying attention, but when she turned her eyes back to the long gravel driveway leading to the mountain road, she realised she'd lost control. She slammed the brake.

The car skidded and with a thunderous explosion of sound, collided with a tree. Birds and bats erupted from the shadowy foliage. Branches and leaves fell. The monster rolled off the roof.

Trog curled into a ball, but he still came to a crunching stop when he hit the next large tree in his path.

Smoke billowed from the bonnet. Aisha checked herself to make sure she was okay, and aside from her heart beating faster than she'd ever thought it could have, she was fine. "Dad?" she asked, scared to hear the answer.

He groaned in pain. "Thank God *you* had *your* belt on," he said. He'd bounced over the back row and collided hard with the passenger and driver seats before rolling into the footwells.

"Can you walk?" she asked.

"I think so. Where's Trog?"

Beyond the billowing smoke, she could see a huge shape moving, climbing to its feet. She fumbled for the gun. "Cover your ears," she said, needing to see if it worked as easily as she thought it did.

She pointed the firearm at the hole Trog had kicked through the roof. She pulled the trigger and the gun blasted. *Okay.*

The huge, silhouetted shape of Trog was moving gingerly, clearly pained by the succession of heavy blows he had received, but when he saw Aisha step out of the vehicle, he bellowed again.

"Fuck you," she said, levelling the weapon square at the creature's barrel-sized chest. She pulled the trigger. Another blast sounded, and the explosion of blood in the top left of Trog's left pectoral muscle told her she'd hit him.

Trog grunted and sat clumsily, sliding down the tree.

Another one to make sure, Aisha thought. She pulled the trigger again, but this time, nothing happened. The gun was empty. *Fuck!*

She opened the back door, and helped Dad get to his feet. He was in a bad way. His face was still pissing blood, and Mum's projectile head had knocked several teeth out. "It's too dangerous out there on the road," she said, knowing they might not be able to flag down a car for ages. "It will be able to track us too easily.

"Go back to the house," he said, retrieving the iron from next to the spare tyre. "With those assholes gone, we can fix the phone and call the cops."

Trog was still slumped at the foot of the tree. She didn't like the fact he was still breathing and wished she had another round. Using the tyre-iron would mean getting close enough to the monstrous beast to bludgeon him. It wasn't a risk worth taking.

"Quickly then. While he's hurt."

The house wasn't far away in the grand scheme of things, but given the yowie's rapid pace, the uphill climb of their driveway, and their bruised and beaten bodies, time was of the essence. Any unnecessary hold-ups could mean Trog was on them before they got there.

Dad limped forward, leading the way.

"Dad, how are we gonna secure the house?" It had gotten in by simply bashing its way through the floorboards beforehand. "It's not like the walls will stop it."

Dad grinned. "We'll cross that bridge when we come to it, but let's just say I have an idea."

CHAPTER SEVENTEEN

In the dark recesses of the passage, at the bottom of the ladder where he'd fallen to a crunching stop, Wolf had pulled himself into a sitting position. All he could remember was a massive *thing* rampaging up the ladder and grabbing hold of him before he could do anything to avoid it. In his head, it seemed like some sort of huge gorilla-type creature, if said gorilla had taken an absolute shitload of steroids and growth hormones. The way it had grabbed him, beaten him against the wall, and thrown him to the ground like so much waste was no joke.

The aches and pains in his entire body made it hard for him to feel around the dusty ground for his flashlight. It had bounced out of his hands when he'd hit the deck. Given the fact he was sure he'd cracked at least a couple of ribs and didn't even know if he could stand up yet, he'd be amazed if the flashlight would even work if he found it. *Still, needs must.*

With his lower back letting him know he would need some proper chiropractic care once all this was done and dusted, he finally rested his hands on the flashlight. He ran his hands up and down it, glad to see it was in one piece. He thanked his lucky stars the people he'd stolen it from weren't the kind to cheap out on Amazon knockoffs and flicked the switch.

The sharp beam of light lit up the passage, showing him just how far down into the ground he was. *Goddamn*, he thought. *If he'd fallen even half the distance, he was lucky he wasn't paralysed.* He used one of the rungs to pull himself to his feet and shone the torch around the four walls.

No. Fucking. Way. One wall was open except for the kind of iron bars you'd see on an old-school zoo exhibit. Not wanting to bring back the wrong memories, he decided not to be reminded of their similarity to prison bars. Jail had been a dark time in his life, and if he'd known snatching an old biddy's handbag would land him a six-month stint in Waco, he'd have worn a mask—and probably not driven away in his own car with his licence plate on display.

The most surprising thing, though, was

the hoarding on top of the prison: TROG THE ANTIPODEAN SASQUATCH. The creature hadn't been a gorilla at all. He didn't know what the hell 'antipodean' meant, but he knew sasquatch meant the monster had been a goddamn bigfoot. He inspected the ladder to make sure it was still sturdy, then grinned. If the thing was still up there, and he could catch it and drive it around the country, showing it off for cash, he'd be rich as hell. *Shit, he might even be able to buy a house and become a pleb like the rest of society!*

He stepped through the broken door and flashed the light around the space. It was old, but it was big, and with a natural channel of water running across the bottom and out through a small crevice in the bottom right, he realised the creature would have had access to water for as long as it needed it. Whoever had built the cage down here had given it plenty of thought.

As the light fell on human remains, he

wondered if he was spotlighting the person who'd locked the upstairs door behind themselves before meeting their demise. Then he saw there were several more piles of human skeletons, and not all of them looked like they'd been scattered and smashed. Some looked like they'd been left in the corner for convenience. Besides them, there was a huge pile of tinier bones, remnants of whatever the sasquatch had killed and eaten. There were so many it was clear this beast, this Trog, had been down here for a long time.

Satisfied with his investigation of the premises, he heard voices carrying in the quiet night air. He'd come down here with someone else. *The Dad!* Somehow the bastard had gotten out of here. And he'd taken the chainsaw! *Motherfucker!*

Wolf looked for something else to use as a weapon but had to satisfy himself with the knife still sheathed in his tactical belt. He grunted. Things could be worse, but it wasn't ideal if he had to fight someone who had a chainsaw.

Approaching the top of the ladder, he climbed more carefully, tried to still his wheezing breath and avoid coughing, not wanting to give away his position. He was going to need the element of surprise. His body was sore, and he wasn't going to be as gung-ho as he'd like.

He knew the smell of copper and death all too well, and as the fresh air at the top of the ladder hit his nostrils, the twin stenches of spilled blood and shit wafted over him. He was in the vicinity of someone who'd died violently. Hopefully it was the dumbass dad. He had been a real pussy and deserved whatever horrible fate he'd met.

When he saw the discarded zombie mask and the complete destruction of zombie's head, he gagged. *Holy shit.* Trog was a fucking savage. Zombie was no pushover, but then Trog would probably be able to take care of a full-grown elephant without too much hassle.

The voices coming up towards the house were familiar. They sounded like the dad and daughter talking. Wolf pulled himself out of the passage and, keeping his flashlight as low as possible to the ground, crawled across to Zombie. Not only was the poor bastard's head a bloody ruin, but the final insult was as crystal clear a warning as Wolf had ever seen: a huge, bloodied footprint was stomped into the ground, and it had filled with blood leaking from Zombie's crushed skull.

Wolf covered his mouth with his inner elbow and held back a gag. *Was Skull still alive somewhere or had she gotten away?* He hoped she'd gotten away. If Dad and daughter were still alive, there was every chance she'd made it too. After all, she had a gun. She could have stopped it in its tracks. He was sure he'd heard firing, so hopefully it was all over and done with.

Just above him, the floor was a ruin.

More blood was smeared across the surface. What looked like bits of hair and skin were smashed across the splintered edges of the broken floorboards. It was hard to tell from the gummed and bloody remains, but the hairs might have been blonde. The mum. *At least one of the fucking normies who lived here must be dead. Good.*

Careful not to put his hands in bloodstains, Wolf pulled himself up through the hole and into a bedroom with the look of a guestroom. The stench of copper death was stronger than ever in here, and it was obvious why. Mum's headless body lay discarded, half-on half-off the bed. The ruin of her neck revealed her head had been pulled off by something with immense force. As he lifted his legs through the gap and climbed to his feet, he saw Mum's stomach had been opened. Her spine was visible through the gap. Intestines were strewn around the room.

The place was a fucking mess.

Pausing, he listened for sounds of danger. The house was silent. Apart from the voices still audible outside, he realised the whole area was devoid of natural sound. If the birds hadn't cleared out, they were keeping quiet. Even the cicadas and insects of the night had shut the hell up. They were clearly smarter than the two humans outside. The thing must be hungry after who knew how long trapped in prison.

Sick of the stench in the room, Wolf made his way back into the living area. There'd clearly been a struggle in there too. Furniture was overturned. There were bullet-holes in the walls. More blood. This job had become a total clusterfuck. He needed to get out of here, but he'd be damned if he went wandering straight outside. There was no sight of Trog's body. He was still a potential threat. Plus, Dad and Daughter were coming this way.

Wolf smiled and repositioned his

mask. He might not have much in the way of weaponry, and he had no idea where his chainsaw was, but the sledgehammer was still resting near the couch and the kitchen was just beyond the door. If the monster didn't get them first, he would.

And then he'd blow their house in.

CHAPTER EIGHTEEN

With his arm around Aisha's shoulder, Garrett limped painfully up the steep driveway. So far there was no hint Trog was following. He pressed forward. His head was killing him. He'd been able to get a good look at his reflection in the car window and hadn't liked what he'd seen. If he came out of this alive, he was going to need severe dental work. His nose was probably broken. He fought back the urge to feel sorry for himself right now, though. His wife had been destroyed by a mythical creature and her head was somewhere in the front yard, waiting to be picked clean by beetles and birds. He had bigger problems than a few bruises.

More importantly, getting Aisha to safety was priority number one, which was why they were heading back to the house. He knew exactly how to stop Trog getting to her, at least for long enough to get the authorities out here. From there, he didn't know what would happen, but he knew he had a lot of making up to do with his daughter.

"I'm sorry, Aisha," he said, squeezing her forearm.

Before he could continue, she hugged him more tightly. "Don't be. It's not your fault."

Garrett gulped. "No, not just about tonight. About everything. About bringing you up here when you didn't want to come. I just thought after everything, I had to make sure you came with me...I always felt like—"

"It's okay. I get it. You wanted to protect us, and you did. I'm sorry I was such a bitch about it. It can't be easy for you to work so far away from us and live alone through the week."

He could feel tears welling in his bruised tear-ducts. "I always felt like being away made you vulnerable; if I was there, none of it would have happened. A dad should look after his family, especially his daughter."

Aisha sighed. "Dad, it's forgiven, and it's not important right now. Patrickson would have done what he did whether you were there or not. You couldn't have stopped it if you tried. He was a sick and twisted jerk-off, and thousands of women whose dads don't work away during the week still have to put up with douchebags like him. It's fucked, but he's behind bars. He's been stopped. It's not your fault, and you need to realise it. You can't wrap me in cotton wool, and in-case you hadn't noticed, you kinda don't need too. In spite of how horrible it was, I've become stronger so I can make sure no one ever puts me in the same position again, and we can't afford to feel sorry for ourselves right now."

As they bridged the apex of the driveway and the house came into view, Garrett paused, thinking he'd heard something in the bushes behind them. He scanned the area, looking for the huge, lumbering shape of Trog, only turning back to the house when Aisha tugged on his arm.

"When it's on us, we'll know. Keep moving," she said, as she assumed the lead position.

Garrett's head was foggy and his body was bruised, but he had enough of his wits left to know Aisha was right. "It means a lot to hear you say those things. I just, I just wish we'd had the conversation before all of this, you know…" he trailed off, not wanting to finish the thought. When Gemma had died this evening, she hadn't had the closure he'd just received. For all she knew, the two of them might as well have died without atonement. The tensions between he and Aisha had bothered Gemma, as they should have. "I guess, I just don't really know whether moving us all up here together was me pretending I was doing it for you, but doing it for myself, or whether I really did think it was best for you because I was scared things might get bad again and I wouldn't be there."

Aisha paused this time. "You know, I was mad at you at first, and you know why. I felt like I'd gotten control of everything when you made us move six hundred kilometres away from our home, from my friends, but when I think about it now, it doesn't matter. We're together, and we're going to get through tonight so we can give Mum the burial she deserves."

Garrett couldn't believe how mature his young lady had become and how much of her life he'd missed due to working

ZACHARY ASHFORD

away. "I just want you to know I love you."

"I know. I love you too. And you know what. Moving us up here might not be the worst thing. If we've got to look for a silver lining, I'm tougher than I ever knew. Now, let's get to shelter and try to see the night through."

The heavy beating of a solid object on a tree trunk and the vicious roar of a blood-crazed predator let them know Trog was ready to pick up the trail. With the house in view, Garrett sped up, pushing through the pain barrier. "Now," he said, "I told you I had an idea. We're heading to the pit. I've a feeling it might be the most secure place on the property."

Keeping pace, Aisha looked at him quizzically. "Are you serious?"

He nodded. They just had to get the length of industrial chain he used to secure tools on the jobsite when he went out on the field. "Trust me. We can keep him out of there."

"Well, let's go," Aisha said. "I'm pretty sure he's not moving at full speed, but he's still probably a lot faster than we are."

CHAPTER NINETEEN

Trog was hurting. The humans had shot him with their painful stinging weapons a few times tonight, and although it had been a long time since the first humans had shot him back when he was captured, he wasn't happy to know the weapons still caused just as much pain as they had back then. Thankfully, none of them had hit him anywhere vital.

His species had thick skin, powerful bony plates protecting their heart from injury, and incredible fortitude due to the nature of life when his species was plentiful. The males would fight for mating partners, for territory, and for resources. Given their propensity to use projectiles and primitive weapons, only those with the toughest adaptations had made it into the breeding stock.

Not that Trog had breeding on the mind right now. The all-consuming thought in his head was blood. He'd gone past the point of hunger. He was fighting for pride and for revenge. These pesky humans had hurt him, but he knew they were hurt also. He knew they were scared, and he liked it. They deserved to have their limbs pulled from their bodies, their faces smashed.

Once he'd torn them to pieces, he'd stash them in his cave, and he'd live off their flesh until he could either find more human prey or he could find his way into one of the big forests he'd known before he was captured. When he was young, the elders had spoken of the humans. At one point, they carved out a respectful relationship with his kind. Then others had come from the sea and brought death and destruction to the land. Now, he would bring death and destruction to *them*. He would repay them for imprisoning him.

He sniffed the air, following the scent of blood and sweat. The male was easiest to smell. His blood was thick in the atmosphere. Trog let loose with another huge growling call of hatred, promising violence on the humans. There was no running from him now, and he wanted them to know it. There was no doubt his voice struck terror in their puny hearts, marinading them with the sweet flavour of fear. He roared again, slapping his thick palm against a nearby tree.

He was coming, and he was intent on blood.

CHAPTER TWENTY

Aisha tried to follow through on her promise to Dad and avert her eyes from Zombie's body, but it was no easy task. She couldn't help but stare at the wreckage of his head when she did finally catch a glimpse of the corpse. The shape of Trog's footprint was now full to the brim with Zombie's blood. There was so much of it, she couldn't fathom how it could all fit inside a human body.

"I told you not to look," Dad said. "I don't care how mature you are, no one is old enough to see that. It can't be unseen."

Too bloody right. Unfortunately, it wasn't the only horrific thing she'd seen tonight. She had no doubt she'd be heading back to therapy to speak some of the nightmarish images through with some poor, unfortunate counsellor who'd look at her with sympathy, pitying her for having to see such things. Aisha smirked. She thought she'd had issues last time she went to counselling. Whoever she spoke to this time was going to have their hands full.

"Why the hell are you grinning?" Dad asked, leaning into the pit where the door used to be and inspecting the base of the ladder.

"Just thought of something funny."

He raised an eyebrow, then went back to what he was doing. "Well, I'm going to burst your bubble, darling. I know you're capable of looking after yourself, but the big prick in the wolf mask isn't where I left him."

Aisha flexed her fingers. Her stomach roiled. "Meaning…?'

"It means he's no longer in the pit, and seeing as we don't know where he is, you're going down there with me right now."

Suspicion flickered. "And are we staying there together?"

Dad gave her the 'you know the answer' face and shook his head. "I'm going to get the phone working again, and no, you're not coming with me."

A huge roar bellowed from somewhere close.

"You'll stay down there with me. We

need to stay together." She'd already come so close to losing him tonight, the thought of letting him go inside the house alone when Trog and the freaky wolf-mask wearing sonofabitch were about didn't rest easy. "And if you won't, I'm coming with you. I'll keep watch for you."

Dad sighed. "I know we just had our big heart-to-heart, clear-the-air talk, but I need you to do what I say on this. If it helps, don't look at it as an ultimatum. Look at is an adult decision you get to make."

Aisha groaned. It didn't matter whether she'd forgiven him or not, the 'make an adult decision' line was one he'd never stop using. She acquiesced.

Dad made sure the cave and prison were empty and told her to hurry down. She climbed to the backdrop of Trog's rhythmic knocking on tree trunks and bellowing rage. "You know, if he finds your old guitar, he could be a singer in those bands you like," she said.

"At least that way he might drink himself to death and leave us alone, right?"

Aisha chuckled softly. She hugged him. "Be quick. I love you and we're gonna get out of this together. Bury Mum."

"See you soon," Dad said. "If I don't come back, don't come out till morning."

Dad scooted to the top of the ladder and disappeared.

Aisha turned to the empty cave. It reeked of acrid urine. The TROG THE ANTIPODEAN SASQUATCH advertising hoarding was situated proudly above the broken gate, looking just as Dad had described it to her. The men who'd captured Trog must have been nuts. She slipped into the cave and looped the chains around the iron bars, wrapping them so tight there was barely any movement in them and padlocked herself inside, trying not to look at the piles of bat bones or human remains. When she killed the flashlight, she was shocked at how dark it was. Yes, it was night-time, but given there had been a door covering this cavern for so many years, she wondered what spending so long in pitch black darkness had done to Trog's sanity. *No wonder he's pissed; he probably flipped out!*

Above the passage leading to her hiding place, Trog roared again.

Aisha froze. The sound of heavy breathing entered the cavern. Trog was coming down the ladder. *Shit.* She slinked back around the side of the cave, away from the door, wanting to remain invisible, wanting to remain still.

Moments later, the sound of Trog's snuffling filled the space. He rattled the gate. Grunted. Rattled it harder.

Aisha held her breath, waiting for the chain to snap. Hopefully, she'd wrapped it tightly enough around the bars to prevent him getting a good grip on it. She'd seen the beast's brute strength on display, and if he could snap spines, pull heads free from bodies, and kick through sheet-metal,

159

snapping a chain shouldn't be out of the question.

He roared. The sound echoed off the cavern walls. Bats flittered about above Aisha's head, and she crouched low, covering her hair. She'd heard they gave you something called Hendra virus. She didn't know what it was, and she didn't want to find out.

Trog rattled the gate more aggressively. Smashed his fist against it. Bellowed.

Aisha curled into a ball and waited for him to go away. In this instance, sitting still and shutting the fuck up was easily the most active and responsible method she had for protecting herself. If Trog got into the cavern, there'd be no escape.

Shouting broke out in the house. *Dad!*

Trog roared again. The ladder rattled as he flew up. Aisha breathed a huge sigh of relief, and then, almost immediately, began to panic again. Her dad was up there, in

Trog's path, and if she didn't get up there to help, there was no way he would make it back down alive.

She recalled his words. "Promise me you'll stay here." She considered them, then decided she couldn't. No responsible adult would. As quietly as possible, she unlocked the chain and followed Trog's path up the ladder.

CHAPTER TWENTY-ONE

Garrett had slipped into the house by going around the back. Avoiding the guest room was an easy choice. There was no way he needed to see whatever state Trog had left Gemma in. It would also be an easy place for Wolf to ambush him. He'd played enough UNREAL TOURNAMENT in his younger days to remember the trap in the submarine level of the Capture the Flag maps. He pictured the masked maniac standing next to the hole in the guest room floor with a fucking flak cannon in his hands. *No thanks.*

Because the rude bastards who'd broken into his house had decided to smash all the windows, he had his choice of entry. He opted for the master bedroom. He had no idea where Wolf would be, but at least the windows were big and open there. This entry also provided him with easy access to the hallway cupboard and toolbox. If he was going to fix the phone, he'd need tools and an easy route in and out of the house.

He slipped through the smashed sliding patio door, careful not to tread on any of the broken glass and give away his location. Slowly, he snuck into the hallway. Again, so far so good. The coast was clear, and he moved towards the hallway cupboard as quickly as he could, grabbing the toolbox. On a whim, he noticed the case of flares he had stashed beside them. He'd never gotten rid of them when he sold his tinnie, assuming they might come in handy at some nebulous point in the future. If worst came to worst and he couldn't get the phone connected, he could fire flares into the sky. Theoretically, they should ensure *someone* investigated their cause.

When he turned to go back the way he'd come, he froze. Wolf sat on the bed, spinning the sledgehammer slowly in his hands. He must have been hiding in the ensuite or the walk-in wardrobe when Garrett came in. "Long time no see," the crazy bastard said. "Been expecting you."

"Makes one of us," Dad said. "I'd hoped you were dead."

"Sorry to disappoint." Wolf rose to his full height. He might have been moving slowly, obviously feeling worse for wear— like Garrett—but he still had an impressive physique. The sledgehammer did nothing to detract from it. He approached the bedroom door with measured steps. The mask added to the menacing effect he created. Garrett gulped. Beating the guy in a fair fight would be hard enough. Going up against him while he was armed with a sledgehammer was not a prospect he relished.

Trog's bellowing shook the house. He was close.

He hoped Aisha had locked herself in. He stepped away from Wolf, not wanting to take his eyes off him. He could escape through Aisha's room, but he'd need to be quick.

"Catch!" He tossed the toolbox underarm, hoping to surprise Wolf. *No chance.*

Wolf blocked the projectile with the hammer. "Nice try, fuckwit." He leapt out of the bedroom and thrust the sledge forward like a spear. There was no room to swing in wide arcs in the hallway, but Garrett continued to back away, nonetheless.

"Pretty rude behaviour for a guest," Dad said, edging up the corridor towards

Aisha's room.

"Fucking die!" Wolf howled, running at Garrett.

The hammer came forward again, surging in a straight and deadly line. Garrett dodged it and tried to grab it with two hands, dropping the flares. He was too slow.

Wolf thrust the hammer forward again. Faster. "Catch this one!"

Somehow, Garrett got two hands on the shaft, but he couldn't deal with Wolf's strength. The big man pulled the hammer in like he was reeling in rope, dragging Garrett with it, and shoulder-checked him as soon as he was within range.

Garrett collapsed to the floor, shaken by the power of Wolf's lunging strike. He scampered, rolled, wriggled, knowing if he stayed in one place for even a second too long, he was likely to be treated to a facelift by sledgehammer for his troubles.

Somewhere close, Trog bellowed.

Sure enough, the hammer came down.

Again, Garrett was grateful there wasn't the space for the big bastard to give it a proper swing. It crunched into the floor, splintering yet another floorboard.

He kicked out, trying to catch Wolf's knee, but only barked his shin instead.

"Prick!" Wolf growled, hopping backwards, but quickly came forward, throwing the sledge out and down, catching Garrett in the midsection.

Thankfully, Wolf's lack of manoeuvrability meant he couldn't get too much power into the blow and Garrett managed to grab the sledge with the tightest grip he could muster. He held onto it, and the two entered a dangerous tug of war, one which would see the winner claim the weapon.

With Garrett's low centre of gravity, Wolf couldn't use Garrett's grip to his own advantage. He howled in frustration and went for the boot.

Garrett grunted as the thick leather toe

crunched into his midsection.

Trog bellowed another terrifying shout of rage. This time, from inside the house.

He must have made it into the guest room already. Which probably meant Aisha was safe. *Thank fuck!* Garrett spun, seeing the monster heading straight for Wolf. He released the hammer and grabbed the flare gun case. *Time to go!*

When Wolf noticed the look on Garrett's face, he checked his shoulder, then started backing off also, keeping pace with Garrett.

Trog growled.

CHAPTER TWENTY-TWO

Aisha came up as quietly as she could, trying not to alert Trog to her presence but also not wanting him to have too much of a head start. If he got to Dad before she did, or if the guy in the Wolf mask had hurt him, she needed to make sure she was following through on her promise to stand up for herself—and the ones she loved. If she didn't, she may as well still be back at home in Brisbane, moping around, feeling sorry for herself.

When she'd gotten to the top of the ladder, she'd heard the yowie moving around in the guest room and Dad and Wolf arguing. She had entered through the front door, not wanting to see Mum's corpse. By the time she got through the lounge room, Trog's bellowing had drowned out all other sounds in the house. When she stepped past the kitchen, taking a view of the corridor, the scene unfolding before her was one of sheer disbelief. Dad was backing away, heading towards her room at the far end of the corridor, and Wolf was swinging the powerful end of the hammer underarm, driving it into the side of Dad's knee as he backtracked.

The knee buckled as Dad screamed.

"Noooo!" *Not Dad too!* She couldn't let him die as well.

She didn't know whether it was her imagination, but even through the grimace of pain on her screaming Dad's face, she thought she saw sadness in his eyes when he saw her there.

Wolf spun. His face was invisible under his wolf mask, but he tilted his head, much like a confused puppy, and swung the huge hammer he'd used to break into the house at Trog, who'd closed the distance between the two men and himself.

The yowie evaded the weapon as it jabbed forward and screamed at Wolf, slapping its chest in a threatening manner and assuming an aggressive pose.

Behind the two combatants, Dad rocked back and forth, clutching his knee, gesturing for her to turn away and exit the house. She froze, unsure how she could help him, unsure if she *could* help him. At this point, she had no idea which of the two threats were most harmful. The yowie could rip her apart, but Wolf was just as dangerous. She had no idea why he hadn't left the house, but she'd be damned if she left Dad here to fight alone. If she couldn't get him out, his death was imminent.

As she debated her options, Dad took matters into his own hands. "Get the fuck out of here, Aisha! You've got to save yourself. Please!"

She clutched her head. Before she could respond, Wolf feinted, throwing Trog's guard in the wrong direction and then redoubled with a backwards movement, driving the hammer into Trog's face with a sickening crunch.

The beast staggered, grabbing the side of its maw with a huge hand, swinging its other arm in a powerful arc, skittling Wolf, sending him crashing to the floor beside Dad.

Trog closed on them.

Aisha thought about the judge when he

asked if Patrickson was the same man who'd been following her, who'd been sending her messages on social media, and threatening her when she ignored his pleas for attention. She'd finally faced him, eye to eye, and said, 'yes, Patrickson was the one who'd made her life a living hell.'

"Hey, Trog!" she yelled, pounding her fists on his back again. She had no idea what she would do if she got his attention, but at the very least, she could buy her father time.

Trog rounded on her, and with an open palm, he slapped her so hard in the chest she went crashing through the kitchen and fell heavily on the stove. Pots and pans rattled. Thankfully, she hadn't tried cooking pizza earlier, but then she remembered her mum's lesson. The gas would run and run if you didn't turn it off properly. *A beautiful fire hazard.*

If she could trap Trog or Wolf in the house, she could immolate them, leave them burning. She flicked the switch, hoping Dad had sorted out his insurance.

She crawled back in Dad's direction.

Trog had grasped Wolf by his shirt, and was lifting him high in the air, clearly outraged the man had hurt him. The two of them struggled, Wolf using the hammer to drive close body blows into the beast, distracting him from doing any severe harm.

"Dad, crawl towards me!"

Dad looked at her, sadness and agony painting his face. He started to pull himself along the floorboards by his hands, grunting and moaning with pain as he moved. His knee was clearly broken. Even from her position in the kitchen, it was twisted at an angle it was never designed to achieve. He slid a case in front of him, pushing it forward like it was the most important thing in the world. Then she realised what it was. When he first got his tinnie, he'd told her she was never to touch it. There were real live explosives inside, and while they were designed to save lives, they could be lethal in the wrong circumstances. Thank God he'd kept them when he sold the boat.

The smell of gas was filling the house now. It reminded her of waiting in the car while Dad got the barbecue gas canister filled at the hardware store, back when they still lived in the old house. She'd give anything to have her old life again, and if Dad could just get close enough, she could drag him out while Wolf and Trog fought.

"C'mon, Dad! Move!"

"Run! Get out!" he grunted through wheezing breaths. "You've got to get out. It's too dangerous!"

Trog, two hands closed around Wolf's head, squeezing, looked down at Dad. He snarled and lifted his big foot.

"Watch out!" she yelled.

Dad looked up just in time, then pressed himself against the skirting board as Trog's powerful foot smashed down into the floorboard, cracking timber.

She ran in, grabbing Dad's arm, not worrying if Trog went for her. She had to get him out.

Trog howled a cry she hadn't heard before. One of pain and shock. She glanced a look in his direction. Wolf had jammed a knife in the monster's eye. The creature was bellowing and howling, clutching the stabbing weapon and doubling over.

Wolf, free of the creature's grasp, raised the upside-down hammer directly above Dad. "Say bye-bye, Daddy."

"No, don't!"

He howled, driving the tool down like a piledriver, smashing it through Dad's feeble block and crunching his face into a paste.

"NOOOO!" Aisha couldn't believe it. She'd been so close to getting him out of the house. She could have saved him if she'd done more. Now she was all alone. Her against the cruel world.

Trog grunted, finally pulling the knife

from his eye and casting it down the hallway. He turned, but Wolf was ready. He thrust the handle of the murderous implement into the beast's side.

Trog grunted again.

Wolf followed with another blow, taking advantage of the beast's lack of sight on its right-side.

Aisha, knowing she had to get the hell out of here, knowing there was nothing left for her in this house, snatched up the flares. "Hey, Wolfie," she said as he readied another blow for Trog.

He turned towards her, again cocking his head like a puppy. "Oh, bitch, you are so stupid."

She snapped out a leg, just like her self-defence teacher had shown her, kicking the big man straight in the balls. She followed through, striking so hard she could imagine his nuts shooting out the back of his skull and bouncing off the ceiling.

He collapsed, holding onto his groin,

whimpering like a beaten puppy.

Aisha didn't wait to see what Trog would do. Flares in tow, she ran, smelling gas in the air. This time, knowing she could face the sight of her mum's corpse, she went through the nearby guest room and jumped through the hole in the floor without looking over her shoulder to see if anyone was following.

She splashed in the pool of Zombie's blood gathered in Trog's footprint and ran for the passageway and the ladder. If her plan wasn't successful, she could lock herself in the prison, secure until the emergency services made it out to the inevitable fire.

From the top of the ladder, she listened for sounds of life. She heard Wolf's screams and Trog's bellows. The creature must have taken advantage of his assailant being knocked off his feet and set about ripping him apart. She had no proof to back up her suspicions, but she thought the yowie might be saving the worst for the one who'd come closest to killing it.

She pulled the flare gun from its case, inserted the flare and, remembering the way Dad had shown her it worked, aimed it at the hole Trog had made in the guest room.

She fired and slid down the ladder, fireman-style.

There was a rush of hot air and a huge explosion.

Debris crashed past her as she rolled into the cage and locked it behind her. Underneath the roar of flames and the subsequent explosions of various flammables in the kitchen, bathrooms, and laundry, she thought she heard howling cries of agony which could only come from a creature as huge and powerful as a yowie.

She had no idea whether Trog was the last one or whether somewhere out there in the ancient primordial forests of this massive country other creatures like him roamed their territories, living as they always had, surviving in the hidden recesses of a land so old its volcanoes had dried up and eroded away.

When the screams of agony finally died, she balled herself into a foetal position and cried. She let the sobs rack her body until there was nothing left in her.

She could feel the heat from the flames as she cried, and she could smell her home burning. Thankfully, despite the scent of it on the air, the smoke didn't seem to be entering the cavern. If she passed out, if the smoke choked off the oxygen coming into the cavern, she was well aware she could die. As it was, all she could do was wait for the sound of sirens, hope the explosion and fire had finished off both Wolf and Trog, and falling debris didn't close the passage off so emergency services wouldn't find her.

After what felt like hours, sirens eventually came into earshot. The sounds of industry and machinery above the cavern meant the fire brigade had arrived. She climbed as far up the ladder as she dared and called for help.

Moments later, torches lit up the crevices in the debris covering the passage and a voice called down to her. "Are you hurt? Don't move, we're coming for you!"

Aisha climbed back down the ladder and slumped against the wall.

Eventually, when the debris was clear, a firefighter made her way down the ladder. Aisha latched onto her and bawled into her shoulder. "Did you find them," she asked?

"What happened here, darling?" the woman responded. "How many were in the house?"

Aisha didn't answer.

"Your mum and dad, were they in the house?"

Aisha nodded. She wiped tears away. "And the others?"

"Five in total. What happened here?"

Aisha counted. *Five? Mum, Dad, Wolf, Skull, Zombie, and Trog.* She shook her head. "Not six? Not Trog?"

The woman looked at Aisha like she was strange in the head. "Trog?"

Aisha pointed to the advertising hoarding. "A big one. A yowie?"

"No, dear," the firefighter said gently. Just five people. Two outside the house, three in it, and all of them in a terrible way. "Did something bad happen here?"

Aisha shook her head. *What a stupid question.* "Of course. Three strangers came. They attacked me while Mum and Dad were out. When they came home..." She broke down into fresh tears.

The firefighter called to her colleagues above ground. "Get the paramedics! We've got a survivor!"

CHAPTER TWENTY-THREE

Aisha scrolled through the feed on her tablet, looking for reports about sightings of the strange creature. Emergency services had only found the bodies of her parents and the home invaders, and although she'd kept pointing out the evidence, the footprints, the DNA potentially strewn around his old prison, the advertising hoarding and the bones of Shackleton and his employees, no one had believed her. Even the doctors and counsellors had thought the yowie was a trauma response, a figment of her imagination invented to help her deal with what they were calling survivor's guilt.

She'd spent a lot of time researching yowies after she'd been released into her Grandma's care, and although she knew people reported seeing them at least a few times a year, she hoped perhaps there would be more sightings around the town of Shackleton, something to prove her story, because if he was still out there, then he was still dangerous.

Trog was insane. All those years in solitary confinement had turned him into a

181

monster with an insatiable taste for human flesh, and as soon as he found somewhere he could once again get a steady supply of it, she knew he would strike again.

"Aisha," Grandma called. "Are you coming down for dinner before the big move tomorrow?"

"Yeah, I'm coming." She switched off her tablet and went down to see what Gran had cooked.

"Are you excited?" Gran asked.

Aisha nodded. After Mum and Dad's funerals, she'd been introduced to an organisation which helped teenagers too big for the foster system set up everything they needed to live independently. For as long as she continued her education, including tertiary studies, they'd cover rental on a studio apartment. It wasn't exactly what she'd meant when she'd argued with Dad about coming back to Brisbane to live on her own, but she knew she had nothing to fear. She knew she had everything she needed inside herself to make it work.

"Yeah, I am," she said. "I think it's going to be good for me."

EPILOGUE

It had taken Trog a long time to heal from his wounds, but thankfully, the many caves around Shackleton had given him somewhere to hide as he recuperated. Most of his fur had been singed off in the fire, but it was slowly growing back, even where mange had affected him before.

Under the cover of darkness, he ventured out into the world, determined to return to the territory he had patrolled before those humans had trapped him so many years ago. Before he could, though, he needed something more filling than rats, bats and lizards to consume.

His journey so far had led him deep into cattle-farming land. He didn't remember there being so many fields here. When he had last roamed this far west, the land had been covered in trees.

Things had obviously changed, but the intrusion of humans on his territory brought with it benefits. From his position in the trees alongside the field, he watched the herd of cattle with his one good eye. Beyond them, a single dim light shone from the human structure past the field.

The cattle lowed. He was downwind from them, and he knew they could smell him, but he didn't care. If he wanted to, he could easily chase one of them down and drag it back into the forest to eat.

Instead, he skirted past them, making his way towards the farmstead. Tonight, he would eat well.